ROYAL HOTTIE

KYLIE GILMORE

Royal Hottie © 2019 by Kylie Gilmore

All rights reserved. No part of this publication may be reproduced, distributed, or transmitted in any form or by any means, including photocopying, recording, or other electronic or mechanical methods, without the prior written permission of the writer, except in the case of brief quotations embodied in critical reviews and certain other noncommercial uses permitted by copyright law.

This book is a work of fiction. Names, characters, places, brands, media, and incidents are the product of the author's imagination or are used fictitiously. The author acknowledges the trademarked status and trademark owners of various products referenced in this work of fiction, which have been used without permission. The publication/use of these trademarks are not authorized, associated with, or sponsored by the trademark owners. Any resemblance to actual events, locales, or persons, living or dead, is purely coincidental.

First Edition: May 2019

Cover design by Michele Catalano Creative

Published by: Extra Fancy Books

ISBN-10: 1-942238-86-X

ISBN-13: 978-1-942238-86-7

Once upon a time there was a swoonworthy prince…

1

———

"Prince Phillip leaves parting gift of a royal jewel after his one-night stands." Ha! Reading the latest headline out loud makes it sound even more ridiculous. Sorry, ladies, my royal jewels *are* the gift.

I'm Prince Phillip Rourke, twenty-nine years old, and second in line to the throne. I have an online following as "the royal hottie" and way, way too many pictures of me rutting my way through Europe with glamorous women. If you read my press, you'll learn my thick dark brown hair is always sexily rumpled, my aquamarine eyes are stunning, and my high cheekbones and strong jaw are classically handsome. Throw in my warm, naturally charming personality and it's easy to see why I'm never lacking for female companionship. Women love me, and I love them right back. Briefly.

I take a sip of scotch, thinking about jetting over to Norway to meet up with Ingrid, a supermodel with as much discretion as skills with her tongue, when my phone rings. I check the screen. Anna, my sister-in-law, the queen of Villroy as of yesterday when she married my older brother, Gabriel, the king. Sadly, my father, the previous king, passed away six weeks before their wedding. He went peacefully in his sleep after a long painful battle with cancer. Anna was the bright spot in his life, and he grew to love her just like the rest of us.

I tap the phone, setting it on speaker on the end table before settling back into my leather club chair in my palace suite. "Anna, I can't believe you're calling me when you're supposed to be on your honeymoon."

She was very enthusiastic about seeing Paris for the first time. Despite living here on Villroy Island for the last three months, right off the coast of southwestern France, she never ventured out for a little sightseeing. She's an American, brash and bold and fun, the near opposite of my brother, a stoic throwback to our Viking ancestors. Fun would have to bite him on the ass, which I guess Anna did. Ha!

Anna's voice carries through the speaker, warm and happy. "We're in the limo on the way to our hotel, and I realized I forgot to tell you something about the guests arriving next week." She's renovated a section of the palace to be used for "the royal experience," either a ladies' week or a honeymoon. It's step one in her plan to bring new jobs and funds to Villroy. This is the first visit, a ladies' week involving all kinds of girly beauty stuff since she's a beautician. Eventually, she plans to build a day spa —away from the palace—featuring beauty products using native ingredients. It's a brilliant idea that will probably save our dying fishing economy.

"What's that?" I ask, already smiling in anticipation. She probably wants me to add something wildly inappropriate to the suite, like edible bikini underwear.

Hmm, some mingling with the lady guests might be in order.

"My dearest clients are super excited for their visit, not just because I'm going to do their hair again. They've missed me at the salon, you know." Her first guests are her wealthiest salon clients from the US.

"Mmm-hmmm." I take a sip of scotch. "You're hard to replace. One of a kind."

"Why, thank you, Phillip. What a sweetheart you are." There's a muffled sound and the gruff growl of my brother Gabriel's voice. He's possessive of his new wife. She gets back to me a long moment later, sounding a little breathless. "What was I saying?"

"You forgot to tell me something about your guests?"

"Oh, yes, and I'm sorry to spring this on you last minute, but I was so busy preparing for my wedding, learning the royal protocol, and supervising the contractors for the guest suite...you know, it still needs a little something. I've got that taken care of as of this morning, so I think we're good to go, but there's always something when you're renovating, especially for a place as old as Amalie Palace. What do you think about renaming it to something like Rourke Palace? It would make more sense at this point since the Rourke family has ruled for centuries, and the French who named it Amalie were from so long ago. I've learned quite a lot of your history—"

"Just tell me." She's usually very direct. The babbling means she's stalling.

"Don't be mad, okay?"

I shift in my seat, suddenly uneasy. "What is it?"

"I promised our guests a bachelor auction to win a date with a prince and, well, you are the royal hottie. That makes you the prime draw. The bidding is going to go sky-high—these chicks are loaded—and we'll funnel the money into phase two, the spa."

I jackknife upright. Knowing Anna, she's going to style my brothers and me in some ridiculous stripper outfits. A real possibility! I put nothing past her. A terrifying vision of a horde of man-hungry women descending on me as I parade around on stage in a shiny silver and blue G-string flashes through my mind. The official royal colors, naturally. And then I'll *have* to go to the highest bidder. No choice in the matter, and I am a choosy man. I expect a certain caliber of sophistication in the women I associate with, not just any woman with a handful of cash. Suddenly, I have an inkling of what Gabriel went through with the barbaric bridal competition my parents set up to find him his bride. A twisted amusing story to those of us not tangled up in it. I laughed at him then. I'm not laughing now.

She continues cheerfully. "So you see, it's all for a good cause."

"Whatever you hoped to make from the bachelor auction, I'll donate to the cause. No, I'll double it." The fact is, the island's economy is one generation away from collapse. The younger generation is leaving in droves, abandoning the dying fishing industry for better opportunities. Our family is well off, mostly in jewels and some well-placed investments, but our money wouldn't be enough to sustain the entire country. I don't mind giving the new venture a boost to start, and so should the rest of the family. Eventually, though, Villroy's economy needs to get there on its own power.

"Actually, it's not the money that's the main purpose of the auction, though, of course, your donation is greatly appreciated. I want my clients invested in their royal experience, knowing the money is going to the day spa, so they'll return when it opens and spread the word about how awesome it is. These women are all very successful in their fields and well connected."

She's really quite savvy and, under any other circumstances, I might appreciate that. Not this time. And what exactly would this date with the highest bidder entail? Some kind of cringe-worthy romantic fantasy? I immediately picture the obligatory stroll on the beach, holding hands, followed by a candlelight dinner, where I'm forced to feign interest in a woman not of my choosing. She'll be giggly over being with the royal hottie or, worse, aggressively trying to get in my bed just for the bragging rights. Not that I would sleep with a woman like that. In the end, I'd come out looking like the bad guy, being labeled as aloof or some such nonsense for having zero interest in my date. And these ladies are here for an entire week. One date may not be the end of it. There could be follow-up lovey-dovey crap.

I scrub a hand over my face. "So we're to be the entertainment portion of the ladies' week."

"Think of it as using your celebrity for a good cause."

She's got me there because I do use my celebrity for good causes. I'm heavily involved with clean water efforts for impoverished countries. *No.* This is different. This is a prince as entertainment. It's beneath me and my title.

"Anna, I'm sorry, but—"

"It will all be very discreet. Only our guests would be there. Please, Phillip, everyone loves the royal hottie. You're famous in America, which makes you the headliner."

I remain firm. "I'm sure when you tell my brothers, they'll be up for it, so you won't even need me." My younger brothers are always up for a good time and don't trouble themselves with princely dignities since they're so far from the throne. "By the way, did you have your guests sign a nondisclosure?"

"Err, no. I keep forgetting that. I'll have them sign one when they arrive. It's possible they told their friends, but don't worry. No one else will be admitted to the palace. This auction is invitation only. Oh, and your brothers already know."

"So everyone knew about this but me?" I bark. And why the hell didn't my brothers tell me? They're still in residence at the palace. Most of my siblings are, though we're all full-grown. It's such a large place we have the privacy of our own suites, and the jet takes us off island whenever we want. I bet they've been laughing their asses off at my expense for weeks.

Anna rushes on. "I've just been so busy, and I happened to run across Lucas, who told Oscar, who told Adrian. Honestly, they're just there as fillers, even though they're just as hot as—ah! *Gabriel!*" He probably pinched her to remind her to look his way for hotness. "Seriously, you're all my guests can talk about."

I am not participating in your damn auction! I clench my jaw to keep from biting her head off. She is, after all, on her honeymoon. She is my beloved sister-in-law. She is the queen.

"No," I say firmly and as politely as possible.

"What? Hello? Phillip, are you still there? Can you hear me?"

I lean toward the phone. "Yes, I can hear you."

"HELLO? *Fffffff*…we're going…tunnel. *Fffff.* I can't hear you!" My brother's deep chuckle carries through the phone loud and clear. "I'll talk to you when I get back." She hangs up.

I jab the button to end the call and finish the scotch in one long swallow. She could definitely hear me. Well, hear this, Anna, queen of Villroy, I refuse to be auctioned off like a piece of meat!

It's been twenty-four hours since Anna informed me of the bachelor auction, and I remain firm in my refusal despite my brothers' attempts to convince me to join them, saying it'll be a blast just like everything with Anna. I shouldn't feel guilty for letting her down. This whole auction business is frigging ridiculous.

I stride to the east wing to take a look at the royal fantasy suite Anna created for her guests, even stepping in with her own tool belt. She was not only a beautician back in the US, but also a handywoman for her apartment building. Is there nothing she can't do? My respect for her won't change my mind about the auction. I understand why she's doing this, but there have got to be better options. I'm hoping visiting the royal fantasy suite will jog my brain into finding that option.

The island is my legacy, after all, where my family has ruled for centuries, our bloodlines dating back to the original tribe of Vikings known as the Wild Ones. My brothers and I loved playing Viking battle when we were kids. Those original Vikings sailed here from an early settlement on the Irish islands, bringing their Irish wives with them. These are my people, this is my island, and—before Anna arrived with her (mostly) fantastic ideas—we were all at a loss as to how to save the economy.

We were once a major seafood supplier, but the fish populations are on the decline and the fishermen have to sail farther out to sea for less catch. Anna's plan involves using the fishing industry to produce cosmetic ingredients —fish oil, sponges, sea salt scrubs, mud, and I don't even know what else. She's preserving our traditional way of life while bringing us into the next century. The woman is brilliant.

My idea to boost the economy—turning Villroy into a destination-wedding venue—didn't go so well. I try not to think about it. Needless to say, the two prestigious magazines in attendance for the inaugural wedding had a field day with the double-booked weddings, one of which consisted of furries. Yes, people who enjoy wearing stuffed animal suits. It was a disastrous event from start to finish, and I'll never live it down. Luckily, Gabriel now sees it as amusing. At the time I thought he might rip my head off with his bare hands.

I stop in front of the royal fantasy suite, surprised to find the door open. The fact that Anna neglected to have her friends sign nondisclosures and they're here early sets off alarm bells. Maybe they've leaked the news already. Maybe the adjoining rooms are filled to the gills with women who can't wait to shout from the rooftops they've been with the royal hottie.

It's quiet. I step inside the living room of the master suite with a balcony that offers a view of the sea. The suite appears to be empty. Maybe a servant was tidying up in here and forgot to close the door. I continue on, stepping into the master bedroom with a four-poster mahogany bed with a sheer white canopy. The furniture in the suite is all antique mahogany with royal blue accents in the upholstery. Local art hangs on the walls, all of it for sale with a discreet brochure for more art available at the Saturday market by the port. Anna has included as many of the islanders as possible in this new venture.

I jam a hand through my hair. How can we help the guests feel invested in this project while maintaining the dignity of the princely title? At least my dignity. My brothers are beyond hope.

"You're Prince Phillip, the royal hottie!" a woman shrieks, startling me. Her accent is American. Definitely one of Anna's friends. She must've been so eager to meet me she arrived a week ahead of schedule. Anna did say I'm all her friends can talk about. I suppress a groan as she steps out of the en suite bathroom, her green eyes huge.

I study her, looking for flaws in the man-hungry woman who wants to bid on me. She's in her twenties, her dirty blond hair up in a ponytail, her skin creamy with a pink flush to her cheeks, pink lips too. She's petite but curvy, maybe five feet, wearing a light blue bohemian-looking embroidered blouse with tight faded jeans and flats. Damn, not a single flaw. She's beautiful. With her hair down, she would probably look even sexier. Still, she has ill intentions, and I must nip this in the bud.

She offers a small wave and flashes a smile that lights up her face. "Hi!"

I frown. "You're early."

"Anna told me to go straight to the royal fantasy suite as soon as I arrived." She shakes her head with a smile. "Sorry I went all fangirl when I first saw you. It's just so weird to see you in real life after seeing so many pictures of you online. You're even better looking in person."

"Thank you," I bite out.

"Something wrong?"

Everything about this situation rubs me the wrong

way. I will not be treated like a piece of meat, even by a beautiful woman who thinks I'm better looking in person. Drawing on every ounce of my royal training, I inform her, "The proper address for a woman meeting a prince for the first time is Your Highness, along with a head bow and curtsy."

Her green eyes widen, her jaw slack.

Normally I wouldn't pull rank, but I can't let her get too familiar, thinking I'm for sale. "You can forget whatever you've been imagining will happen between us. I won't go on a date with you for any price."

Her head jerks back, her brows shooting up. "Excuse me?"

I cross my arms. "You heard me. I am not for sale." I jerk my chin toward the door. "Maybe you should just leave if that's your expectation."

Her eyes narrow, and she doesn't make a single move to leave.

We have a staredown that goes on uncomfortably long. I can't be the one to leave. I've already pulled rank. She must go.

Finally, I break the silence, maintaining unblinking eye contact. "You may go now."

"I'm not going anywhere. Do you know who I am, *Your Highness*?" She says Your Highness in a mocking tone with no requisite head bow or curtsy. Incredibly rude.

"You're one of Anna's friends, which is why I know what you're thinking. You've probably been ogling my picture online, creating fantasies of us riding off into the sunset together or some such nonsense—"

She holds up a palm. "Let me stop you right there. I'm here at the queen's request and, last time I checked, queen trumps prince, so adios, buckaroo. Don't let the door hit your royal ass on the way out." She pulls a tape measure from her back jeans pocket, turns her back to me, and begins measuring various distances in the bedroom—dresser to ceiling, dresser to floor, dresser to bathroom door.

I stare at her in shock. Have I been dismissed? How insulting. I'm second in line to the throne! Why, just three months ago I almost took Gabriel's place as heir when he thought he wouldn't be allowed to marry Anna, a commoner. Dodged a bullet there. I would've done it out of love for my brother, who fell so hard for Anna he was ready to abdicate the throne to have her, but I'm glad to remain the carefree spare. Still, the spare is important. Should anything happen to Gabriel, I will be king, which means I am not to be dismissed!

She pulls a small notepad and pen from another jeans pocket and scribbles for a minute.

I clear my throat loudly.

She glances over her shoulder. "You're still here?" She tucks the notepad and pen away. "C'mere, make yourself useful and help me measure the length of the room." She holds out the end of the tape measure to me.

I turn on my heel and leave, dismissing *her*.

I'm barely two steps out the door when I hear her say loudly to herself, "Boy, the royal hottie sure believes the hype. What a disappointment."

Another insult. I turn back, ready to blast her. *No.* She's not worth even one more minute of my time.

I head back to the west wing to my suite. I'm glad she's disappointed, whoever she is. I didn't even catch her name. Normally I'm warm and friendly, especially with a beautiful woman, but this looming bachelor auction has me on the defensive.

You know what? This is good. Maybe I'll disappoint all of Anna's man-hungry guests and then no one will care that I'm not in the auction. In fact, I'll text Anna right now. *Met one of your guests and I've disappointed her so much she has no interest in bidding on me.*

No response from Anna.

I can't help hammering home my point. *I told you no about the auction, so tell these women to stay away from me.*

By the time I reach my suite, Anna's alarming reply pops up: *That is my friend Ruby. She's doing me a huge favor with a rush interior design job to make the royal suite magical. What did you do?*

Err…

My thumbs fly over the keypad. *I thought she wanted to bid on me. Don't worry. I'll correct the mistake and win her over with my charm.*

Anna: *Don't even think about hooking up with Ruby! She's not into casual sex and doesn't have time to fool around.*

I wasn't thinking that. Though she is beautiful.

Your rep precedes you. We need her, and I can't afford to have you screw it up like you do with every other woman.

Ouch. *Duly noted.*

I love you, just keep it in your pants.

I roll my eyes. *Got it. Ruby is forbidden.*

And since when has the forbidden ever been tempting? Ha. I can control myself. No problem.

2

____

Ruby

Arrogant? Check.

Rude? Check.

Full of himself? Check times a gazillion.

What is his problem? Coming in here, where I'm trying to do my job, and telling me to leave? Informing me he wouldn't go on a date with me for any price? Uh, hello! Did I *ask* him on a date? The guy so believes the hype he can't imagine anyone *wouldn't* want to go on a date with him. *Ooh, I'm the royal hottie.* Get over yourself. Like I want to be his flavor of the week. Geez. I've spent the last two months recovering from a disastrous long-term relationship, which led to losing my job and moving in with my parents. Not where I want to be at twenty-five years old. A playboy like him is the very last thing I need.

I'm not saying he's not gorgeous; he totally is with thick dark brown hair, striking aquamarine blue eyes, high cheekbones with hollows under them, a strong jaw, and full lips. His five-foot-eleven frame is muscular perfection from his wide shoulders to his bulging biceps, barrel chest, narrow hips, and thick muscular legs. Okay, so I'm one of his fangirl followers. I might have memorized his stats and/or ogled his shirtless self on the beach with his current supermodel girlfriend. It was fun to fantasize about the playboy prince. Now that's all out the window because the reality is he's an arrogant rude full-of-himself prince. *Hmph.*

This interior design job is a golden opportunity and one I don't take lightly. When Anna called me on Sunday morning to offer me the job, I got myself on the next flight out. She's reimbursing me for the travel expense in my paycheck too, knowing I'm broke. She's the real deal, a loyal true friend, and I don't find it much of a stretch to call her queen. Her mother-in-law stepped down as queen on her husband's death and is now a princess again.

Anna has already done a wonderful job choosing the furniture, bedding, and draperies. I'm just adding the final touches. The only issue is there are few local island resources for what I need—lighting, decorative accessories, a new fireplace mantel for the master suite—and I'm hampered in working with the closest place to shop, France, by the fact that I speak zero French. Also, I'm on a nail-biting deadline—only one week until her guests arrive. Wait, what time is it here? I'm so thrown off by the time zones. The guests arrive next Sunday night, and it is now plus six hours from East Coast time…Monday afternoon local time. Great, I actually only have *six* days.

Breathe!

First, I need more art. I grab the art brochure with information on the artists who did the suite's paintings. I need to track down these people. I head back to my room one floor up from here and call the servants' quarters for my maid, Maya. We met earlier. She's close to my age and we got along well. I've decided she'll be my ally in finding everything I need. Heck, for all I know she speaks French. Many on the island are bilingual, though English is the official language. Wouldn't that be great?

Maya arrives in a shockingly speedy time, knocking on the open door. Her dark brown hair is in a neat bun, and she wears the servant's uniform of white shirt and black pants.

"Come in, Maya. Thanks for coming so quickly."

She bobs her head. "What can I get you, ma'am?"

"By any chance do you speak French?"

"No, ma'am."

"Do you know anyone who does?"

"The men who work with the horses and the chef."

I consider this. I feel like I'd be taking them away from work that's important to the palace, and they probably would be zero help with decorating stuff. "Okay, no worries." I grab the art brochure and hand it to her. "Where can I find these people? I want to buy more local art."

She scans the names and looks up at me, regret in her eyes, her lips turned down. "Ma'am, most of the artists on this brochure are also fishermen. They're already out to sea. A few might appear at the Saturday market."

"That's very late. Anna's guests arrive on Sunday."

She brightens. "Actually, I know a woman who does murals who might be available. She did the local nursery school's walls with fairy-tale scenes."

"Ooh, yes! I could have a central ceiling painting in the master suite living room featuring a fantastical sea scene with mermaids and sea nymphs. And for the bathrooms, a painted starry sky framed to look like a fake skylight right over the whirlpool tub. Do you know someone local who paints canvases that might be available right away? I could use them for the fake skylights."

She studies the brochure for a moment. "We could try Jeanne. She paints on all kinds of surfaces."

"Great!" My brain starts cranking with the logistics. If I have to, I could skip the bathroom paintings and do something with pinholes of light through a dark fabric for a fake skylight. I suddenly realize Maya is talking.

I refocus on her. "What's that?"

"Do you need me for anything else, ma'am?"

"Actually, I need you for everything. Could you be my personal island guide and help me all week with the interior decorating in the royal fantasy suite? You could be my assistant."

Her hand goes to her throat. "I don't know anything about interior design, ma'am. I'm here to serve our honored guest."

"This is how you can serve me. Please. I can't do it alone, and I only have six days. I don't want to disappoint the queen."

Her brown eyes widen. "Oh, no, me either. Let me check if it's okay and then I'm happy to assist."

I throw my arms wide. "Thank you!"

She blushes and smooths her hair back. "Just a moment, ma'am." She goes to the phone and has a quick whispered conversation. I hear "Her Majesty, the Queen" thrown in a few times and then she turns to me. "All set! Where should we start?"

"We're going to visit with the artists, and then you and I are going shopping at the palace!"

She gasps. "You can't shop here. Nothing is for sale."

"We're borrowing. Stick with me and you'll love the results."

"I don't know, ma'am. Everything has a place."

"Do you have an attic here?"

"Yes."

"Fantastic!"

She shakes her head and then quickly covers with a smile. "As you wish, ma'am."

The artists' visits went well. They're thrilled to be paid for their art. I have a limited budget, but art is always worth the extra. One of them, Clara, is already busy sketching out fantastical sea ideas for the ceiling mural. She'll arrive at the palace tomorrow and I'll arrange for scaffolding for her project. Jeanne had the genius idea of painting the starry sky on a paintable acoustic panel, and she had extra panels from a previous project. This will make both a fantastic fake skylight and add to the hushed romantic feel of the luxury bathrooms. Sometimes spacious bathrooms can echo.

Maya and I have been scouring the dusty attic for hours. It's huge! The entire length of the east wing and there's another attic over the west wing. I found an antique tabletop clock, dull brass candlesticks that we'll get shining in no time, and a vintage 1920s white desktop phone with rotary dial—does it work? Who cares! It looks amazing. I also found a fireplace mantel with chipped paint that's crazy cool. The top of the mantel is in the shape of a crown with a faded royal crest in the center. The royal crest—a lion wearing a crown with the sea and a fish beneath—is awesome too. I'll get the paint touched up on it.

I follow Maya back downstairs, covered in dust. We're

a mess, but it was so worth it. I've got the clock in one hand and the phone in the other. Maya's got an armful of candlesticks. We'll need some help for the mantel, which is too heavy and unwieldy for us. Maya opens a door out to the hallway and immediately drops into a low curtsy. "Your Highness."

It's the royal hottie himself. His crisp white button-down shirt is open at the throat, exposing tanned chest. Dark gray pants with black leather shoes complete his *GQ* outfit.

"Maya!" he exclaims. "I almost didn't recognize you. Have you been sweeping out the chimneys? I'm pretty sure that's not in your job description." Even his accent is sexy, proper English with a hint of French lilt to it. He smiles, his aquamarine eyes sparkling playfully. He is *breathtaking*. I wish I were immune.

Maya blushes. "No, sir. I've been in the attic."

Phillip glances at me and then back to Maya. "It's a nightmare up there. Next time tell me what you need and I'll have it brought down for you. Hold on." He leans close to her and then carefully picks a long cobweb out of her hair, crumpling it in his hand.

Maya looks suitably freaked that something weird was in her hair. "What was it?"

"Just a cobweb."

She holds herself very still. "Any spiders?"

Phillip inspects her hair. "Let me see." He makes a big show of looking all over her head. "Ah. Don't move a muscle."

Maya squeaks.

Phillip laughs. "Kidding!"

Maya laughs too. "Oh, you!"

He looks over at me, still smiling, and my stomach dips. "Hello."

"Hi," I manage because when he's not being an arrogant jerk, he's hot as fuck.

He turns back to Maya. "Is this a new maid, or have I not been paying attention?"

I must have more dust and dirt on me than I realized if he doesn't recognize me. Though I did change my clothes to old ratty sweats, put my Rays cap on, and traded my contacts for glasses. I knew this would be dirty work and I wanted to cover up as much as possible.

Maya shakes her head. "Sir, this is our honored guest, the queen's friend Miss Ruby Evans. She's an interior designer and is putting some magic into the royal fantasy suite." She turns to me. "Right? Magic?"

I smile. "Yes. That's right. It's in my job description per Queen Anna."

Phillip's eyes narrow as he gives me a once-over. "We met earlier." He frowns. "You look different."

"Would this help?" I hang my tongue out and pant. "Remember me now? The one who panted after you, desperate for a date you'd never give me at any price?"

Maya gasps.

Red creeps up Phillip's neck. "Yes. I mean no. Good day." He turns to go.

I stifle a laugh. "We could use a hand getting a fireplace mantel down from the attic."

He stills and turns back to me, which I give him a lot of credit for, considering his neck is still red.

I incline my head toward the attic. "It's leaning against the wall when you first go up. I left a pink Post-it on it. The mantel is white, shaped like a crown at the top with the royal crest. Could you have someone bring it to the fantasy suite?"

And then he surprises me by striding straight to the attic door and heading upstairs to get it himself. What a prince! Ha-ha.

Then I realize he's going to ruin his expensive white dress shirt with the dusty mantel. I set the clock and phone on the floor and holler through the open attic door. "Phillip, wait! You're going to ruin your white shirt. It looks custom-made. You should change or get someone else to help with the mantel."

"No problem," he says, rapidly unbuttoning the shirt. "Wait right there."

I suck in air. I expected him to change not strip. But do I call a halt to the increasingly spectacular reveal? Uh, no. He must have a personal trainer. It's tanned chiseled muscle as far as my ogling eyes can see, from defined pecs to what I swear is an eight-pack with a deep V at the waist. My mouth goes dry as he descends the stairs, his blue-green eyes locked on mine. By the time he's standing two steps above me, my body hums with lust, my pulse thrumming through my veins, and I'm flushed hot from head to toe. He smells intoxicating, like fresh soap, hints of ocean, and sexy man. No, *arrogant* man. *Stay strong.*

He quickly undoes the cuffs, pulls the shirt off, and places it in my hand. "Thank you for your concern, Ruby."

"Yes," I croak. "You're welcome. Any time."

He arches a brow, a sexy smirk on his lips. The bottom lip is fuller than the top, and I'm fixated on it.

He turns and goes upstairs and, oh my God, the back view is incredible—powerful rounded shoulders, muscular back, tight ass. I tell myself there's no harm in looking, even at a rude arrogant playboy prince, as long as he doesn't know I'm looking.

He glances over his shoulder at me. Busted!

My cheeks flame, and I rush out the attic door, his shirt clutched in my hand.

"Ma'am?" Maya asks with some alarm. "Is that His Highness's shirt?"

I clear my throat. My cheeks are still hot. Embarrassment? Lust? Maybe both. "Yes."

"Perhaps we should call for another shirt for him?"

I glance down at the dusty clock and phone I need to carry and his white shirt, which I'm trying to keep safe. "He knows where to find us. I'll…" What will I do? We're both too dirty to carry the shirt or wear it. I look around the hallway and spot a bronze bust at the end perched on a marble pedestal. "I'll just set this over on that bust for him and we'll be back in business."

"But, ma'am, that's the bust of a former king. One of his revered ancestors."

"Then it will suit him."

I walk briskly down the hall and set the shirt over the bust, which, by the way, is completely dust-free. Problem solved.

3

Phillip

This mantel has seen better days, which is why it was in the attic in the first place. I admit I normally wouldn't act as moving man, but I was thrown off by Ruby, who was unrecognizable from before. Her hair was tied back and covered by a dusty Rays cap, smudges of dirt on her tortoiseshell glasses hid the bright green of her eyes, and her body was swallowed up by a baggy gray tracksuit. She surprised me looking like that, and then reminding me of our earlier encounter. I admit I took my shirt off just to give her something else to remember me by.

I know, I know, that was bad form after Anna declared Ruby off-limits, but it's not like I'm going to do anything. It shouldn't be too difficult to keep my distance. Ruby's only here for a week, and I'm leaving very soon. First for a tour with Global Sun Water, a nonprofit I've been involved with for years, and then my travels continue as the new UN Ambassador for Clean Water. I volunteered for the UN position, citing my work with Global Sun Water bringing solar water-pump technology to impoverished communities. Despite my sometimes salacious press, the UN accepted me. The truth is, good or bad, everything I do gets attention in the press, which will subtly put pressure on foreign governments to make clean water a priority. I've committed to the UN position for a year, but they hope I will continue for longer.

Guess what, ladies, I'm not just a pretty face. I want to help with clean water efforts, and I also want to improve my public image for the sake of my family. I've sworn to my grieving mother to keep the scandal to a minimum and stop tarnishing the family name during this critical transitional time for Villroy's monarchy after my father's passing. My mother is in such a deep state of grief she's shut herself off from palace life, only coming out when she absolutely has to. But she keeps tabs on things. I'm not saying I'm taking a vow of chastity, just that I'll be more discreet.

As I approach the master suite, I can hear Ruby and Maya's conversation floating out to the hall. "Prince Phillip is usually very nice," Maya says.

Why, thank you, Maya. She's only three years younger than me. We practically grew up together since her mother worked at the palace too.

"Nice *looking* maybe," Ruby replies. *Maybe?* "I'm telling you he was incredibly rude to me before."

I speed up. I need to defend my honor and put things right. Also, I don't want Ruby to tell Maya the details of our encounter, which the servants will have a field day with.

Ruby's voice rises. "I mean, I didn't ask him for a date and he acted like I was going after him. Do I look like a desperate woman?"

"No, ma'am," Maya replies solemnly. I can hear the

smile in her voice. She has a good sense of humor, though she will always remain professional.

I step into the living room of the master suite and set the mantel against the hearth. They're in the bedroom.

Maya goes on. "Maybe it's because of Queen Anna's—"

"I'm afraid we got off on the wrong foot," I say, appearing in front of them. If Ruby doesn't already know about the auction, I'd prefer to keep it that way. No sense giving her more ammunition against me after our earlier embarrassing encounter. I'm hoping she'll be gone before the auction happens. Besides, I won't be participating in it, and I think that will disappoint her. Not because she wants to bid on me, that's for my sister-in-law's wealthy clients. Ruby will be disappointed that I let her friend, the queen, down.

They freeze, both of them staring at my bare chest. I get that reaction a lot. Good to know my workouts are still massively effective.

I hold my hand out to Ruby. "I'll take my shirt."

"It's out." She points toward the door. "Out there."

Maya drops her eyes to my shoes. "It's on the bust of King Carl the first, in the hallway where we were previously, Your Highness." That's my great-great-great-great-grandfather, who reestablished the Rourke family as rulers two centuries ago, wresting control of Villroy from the British, who'd wrested it from the French, who'd taken control from us, the original Viking-Irish tribe. He is, in a word, a legend. And now he's wearing my shirt. Sacrilege, using my revered ancestor as a laundry hamper.

I rub my temple. "Maya—"

"I'll have it brought round." She rushes to the phone, probably to call the servants' quarters.

Ruby bites her lip. "I was just trying to keep the shirt pristine."

I incline my head toward the living room. Maya's back is to us, but I'd like even more privacy.

She points toward the other room. "You want me to—"

"Yes."

I head to the living room and take a seat on the plush blue sofa in front of the hearth. Ruby appears in the room, looking concerned. We definitely got off on the wrong foot. I pat the cushion next to me. "Please have a seat."

She shakes her head. "I'm way too dirty for that sofa, and I won't be stripping, unlike some exhibitionists I've only just met."

I smile. "I admit I was trying to distract you from your first impression of me. I was worked up about something else, and I took it out on you. I'm sure you must think I was terribly rude. Can we start over?" I offer my hand. "Hello, I'm Phillip. Welcome to Villroy."

She smiles a little and closes the distance between us, standing in front of me. "Hello, Phillip. I'm Ruby and quite happy to be here doing this job for my good friend Anna." She tucks her much smaller hand in mine and I clasp it. My nerve endings flare to life at the touch, surprising me.

Our gazes collide in a moment of shared recognition. Attraction. Chemistry. It's arcing between us like electricity. I give her a brief handshake and drop my hand from hers.

She takes a step back.

"So," she says at the same time as I say, "Ruby."

"You go," we say at the same time and laugh.

She raises a palm. "Prince trumps commoner. Please, what were you going to say?"

"I don't think in those terms. I know the circumstances of my birth were dumb luck. Some people are born into royalty; some born into poverty. I'm simply a lucky man."

She wags a finger at me. "Not as arrogant as I first thought."

I put a hand to my heart. "You wound me." I lean forward. "Though I suppose I deserve it."

She waves that away. "No worries on this front. I'm not looking for a relationship or even a date. In fact, I'm pretty much turned off by your entire species. I might try the softer side. At least women I can understand."

I'm speechless.

She barks out a laugh. "Kidding! Not that there's anything wrong with that. Whatever floats your boat, right?"

"Oh. Ha-ha. Yes."

She shakes her head, smiling. "So let's be friends. Is that where you were going with this?"

I take her in, still looking very much the dirty urchin. She even has smudges of dirt on her nose and cheek. Her petite curves are completely hidden by the baggy gray tracksuit. There should not be a single ounce of temptation in the picture she makes, yet I know we cannot be friends. I felt that chemistry. I need to keep my distance.

"I'm glad we cleared up our earlier misunderstanding," I say formally. "I assured Anna I would make amends."

Her face falls, her gaze dropping to the floor. "Ah. Yeah, sure." She lifts her chin, her earlier open friendly expression now closed. "All cleared up."

I ignore the dull ache in my chest. "Good."

Albert, one of our oldest servants, with thinning white

hair, steps into the room. "Your Highness, I've brought you your shirt."

I stand and take the shirt he holds out to me with a knobby hand. "Thank you, Albert." I put the shirt on, quickly buttoning it.

He bows his head and takes his leave.

Ruby turns and heads back to the bedroom without another word.

Maya's voice carries loud and clear. "I told you he was nice, ma'am." She must've been eavesdropping, like all of the servants.

"Enough about him," Ruby says sharply. "Now let's get to work."

I walk out the door, my limbs heavy. I did what I had to do. No reason for regrets.

~

Ruby

The next day I get the artists, Clara and Jeanne, settled in to do their work. Then Maya and I head out to catch the next ferry to Nantes, France, on a shopping expedition. I'm not sure what I'm looking for, exactly; I'll know it when I see it. Something that would complement the existing decor, bringing a pop to it or an extra layer of regalness. We shall see.

"Maybe Prince Phillip could help us, ma'am," Maya says as we head downstairs. "He was helpful yesterday with the mantel. If we find a large item, we might need him to carry it."

Gah. Phillip. He totally gave me the brush-off yesterday. Apparently, I'm not worthy of his friendship. Add haughty to his list of sins, which I reviewed last night when I found myself replaying our shirtless encounter. No amount of sexy good looks can make up for being a playboy prince who is full of himself, arrogant, and haughty. I've removed rude from the list after his apology. Still…let's add a few more sins for good measure. He's too formal, cocky, and shallow. Oh, yes, he knows he's good looking. He's all about the looks the way he stripped down in front of me. Definitely not my type. I am officially unfollowing the royal hottie.

I look over at Maya. "By that logic, we could get any man with big shoulders to go with us. Forget it. Men hate shopping."

"I'm sorry, ma'am. It was not my intention to overstep."

"What do you mean?"

She's quiet, and I follow her gaze to where Phillip is standing, waiting for us at the bottom of the stairs. My breath quickens, my heart hammering. I will myself to calm the frick down. His dark brown hair is rumpled a bit like he ran his fingers through it, and he's got sexy scruff on his jaw. He's wearing a gray button-down shirt with the sleeves rolled up to his elbows, revealing corded muscular forearms, along with black pants, a thick leather belt, and loafers. He looks casual, like a regular guy I might meet in real life, not this alternate reality I've stepped into for my short visit to the palace. Two badass-looking men stand behind him dressed all in black—blazer, T-shirt, and pants. His security detail. I can tell by the wireless earpieces they wear and their stone-cold serious expressions.

"Good morning, Maya and Ruby," Phillip says warmly. As if there was no haughty brush-off yesterday.

Maya dips her head and curtsies. "Good morning, Your Highness."

"Good morning, Phillip." I can't bring myself to say Your Highness. It feels too much like he's above me, and he's not. "I'm surprised you want to go shopping with us."

"Shopping?" He turns to Maya in mock surprise. "You told me I was to receive an award."

Maya blushes and shakes her head. I suspect she has a crush on him. Even I know a prince wouldn't date his maid. That only happens in the movies.

"No?" he asks in a teasing tone. "I'm not to receive the award for best karaoke?"

Maya laughs.

"What about best example of drunk dancing ever seen in the island's history?" He winks at me, and I shake my head, fighting a smile. He's teasing Maya, and she's loving all the attention.

"You are a fine dancer, sir," Maya says with a laugh.

He inclines his head. "Thank you. Good to know I've at least got that to fall back on. And today I'll play your moving man, shopping assistant, or interpreter, as the case may be."

Maya beams at him and turns to me. "He speaks French."

"That could be helpful," I say, playing it cool. I'm not a blushing maid so easily taken in by a little flirty charm. "I mean, the other stuff is great too. So, okay, let's go."

We head through a side exit of the palace, where a couple of black Mercedes with tinted windows are waiting. Phillip holds the car door open to the backseat. I'm not sure if it's me or Maya he's expecting to sit there. Where do the guards sit?

"You go, ma'am," Maya says. "I'll take the front seat."

I brush past Phillip, his heat close enough to warm me, and murmur, "Thank you," before taking my seat.

He joins me a moment later in the backseat. "Security will take the lead car. There's not much concern here on the island, but they're helpful in public."

There's space between us. Even so, his fresh clean scent washes over me, making me want to lean closer just to breathe him in. *Nice, Ruby, you're turning into the panting desperate woman he thought you were.* No wonder he's a playboy. His pheromones are lethal.

The car smoothly drives down the curving palace road. I take in the gorgeous view of sparkling blue-green sea and bright blue skies with white fluffy clouds. It's near the end of September and the weather is still a comfortable seventy degrees. Why did Phillip volunteer today? Did he do it as a favor to Anna, wanting to help with the royal fantasy suite? Or did he change his mind about spending time with me as a friend? I don't think princes go shopping just to help out their maid.

I stealthily check out Phillip in profile—his expression is neutral. My gaze follows the line of his square jaw, his full lower lip, the cord of his neck, his wide shoulder, back up to—

Crap! He winked at me.

I face front, willing my blush to go away. Busted times a zillion. Augh. I am the worst kind of hypocrite, blaming him for being into his looks and then checking him out. Okay, back to work. Logistics, lists, tight schedule. It's no use. My mind is static. I fear he short-circuited it.

I finally cool off enough to risk a look at him. He gives me a small smile, and I smile back. I'm genetically incapable of not smiling back. I can't help it. I'm a smiler.

Before my crash and burn with Satan, aka my ex, I used to be known for having lots of positive energy. I've been compared, in a good way, to a happy pixie with my petite size and energy.

I attempt a normal friendly tone with Phillip in line with today's agenda. "Will you be mobbed by paparazzi?" That could really hamper our shopping progress.

"I hope not," he replies.

"Let me hear you speak some French."

"Why?"

"Because I want to hear if you sound fluent."

A smile plays over his lips. "And you would know this how? Maya says you don't speak French."

"I've got an ear for language."

"Oh, really? And what languages do you speak?"

"Err, English. But I can recognize a bunch of them."

"How useful." His tone is droll, and I can't help but laugh. He holds up a finger. "*Je ne peux pas manger les produits laitiers.*"

Maya giggles.

"Why're you laughing?" I ask, leaning forward to Maya. "That sounded like real French."

"It was, ma'am," she replies. "It's the one phrase I know. Phillip taught me."

Phillip takes on a mock aggrieved tone. "Did you think I spoke fake French?"

I lean back in my seat. "Well, I don't know. Some people exaggerate their skills."

He huffs and leans forward. "Maya, have I ever exaggerated my skills?"

She beams back at him. "No, sir. You excel at everything."

I lean forward. "He's going to get a big head if you

keep saying stuff like that."

He turns back to me and grins. We're unexpectedly close and my breath catches, the air buzzing between us. His voice is husky. "There you have it."

I lick my lips, surprised at how much I want to close the distance between us. My libido has been in deep freeze for two months for good reason, and now it dances for him. My libido is an idiot.

I sink back into my seat. "So what was that fancy French you said? What did it mean?"

His eyes sparkle with amusement. "I can't eat dairy products."

I laugh. "For real?"

"Yes, for real. Though I can eat dairy products. I said that for Maya. She's lactose intolerant."

"Sadly, it's true," Maya says.

Phillip gestures toward her with a smile. My lips curve up automatically, and I remind myself sternly that this is a business trip. This is my first big job in my new solo interior design business after losing my job at the Happy Mouse Kingdom in Orlando two months ago. I'd like to say I quit, but the truth is they let me go because I wasn't performing at the expected level and there was a waiting list for my job. I lost my mojo, plain and simple. No energy, no creativity, nothing. That's what happens when you find out the man you were living with for a year— madly in love—is married with triplets on the way.

Cue downward spiral.

We met at a club and he treated me so special I fell hard. He lavished me with affection, surprised me with little gifts like my favorite chocolate truffles or flowers for no reason at all, and the sex was hot. Then after a year of blissful ignorant happiness, he informed me I had to move out because we were living in his parents' vacation condo and they were coming for a visit for the upcoming birth of his triplets. He actually expected me to be happy for him.

All I could do was hole up in my old bedroom at my parents' house with its pink and white striped comforter, stuff my face with chocolate truffle ice cream, and hate-watch home decorating shows for being unrealistic. After a while, I scraped myself off the ice-cream-stained bed, pulled together a résumé, and blasted it out. Big lot of nothing. So I went out on my own. I got a few nibbles on the job front, small jobs mostly, redoing a sunroom kind of jobs that cover half a week's rent. Not enough for me to move to my own place, which is necessary because guess who else is pregnant? No, not me. My mom! It's her miracle baby. I was shocked when she told me last month because, after having me, she had a series of miscarriages, and the doctor told her to stop trying for her own health. She didn't think she could get pregnant at forty-three (she had me when she was eighteen). Anyway, Mom's pregnancy with a baby girl (yay!) is going well, and soon my parents will need my room for the baby. I won't move far though. This is the little sister I've always wanted, and I definitely want to be part of her life.

So enough with the male distraction. This job is the key to getting back on my feet, and I won't let a charming smile, intoxicating manly scent, or sexy scruff stand in my way.

I turn to Phillip in full professional mode. "Have you ever shopped in Nantes before?"

"Of course, it's right next door."

"Tell me everything."

Phillip doesn't disappoint, filling me in on the historic le Passage Pommeraye, one of the original shopping malls dating from 1843, to the best places for antiques, clothes, and jewelry. He's unfamiliar with design stuff, but that's okay because he can ask around to get what we need.

By the time we get to the port, I'm convinced Maya did the right thing asking Phillip along, even though I initially thought we wouldn't need him. I step out of the car and spot the ferry already waiting at the side of a long dock. It's filled with passengers.

I speedwalk toward the ferry. "Hurry! We don't want to miss it."

A large warm hand wraps around my wrist, stilling me. I look up into Phillip's eyes—I swear they match the sea here—and the heat in them brings all my nerve endings to life. I felt it when he shook my hand yesterday, too, like an electric current. There's a shimmering attraction between us that I instinctively know will ignite given the smallest push.

I gulp, caught in his grip literally and lustfully.

"This way," he says, giving my wrist a small tug toward the other side of the dock. Maya is already being helped aboard a sleek white yacht.

He releases my wrist and I return to my sensible self. I should've known a prince wouldn't travel crammed onto a public ferry. "Your royal yacht?"

"My royal yacht." His voice drops to a husky drawl. "I promise a smooth ride."

I narrow my eyes at his innuendo despite the obvious chemistry. Yesterday he acted above me; today he's using his charm for what? Seduction? I don't need a man like this, I really don't, even if I do admire him shirtless. And with his sleeves rolled up. And all the time...shit. What the hell is wrong with me? My hormones are out of control. *Down, girl.*

"Isn't it lovely?" Maya calls from the deck.

"It's gorgeous!" I yell back. Then I tell Phillip under my breath, "She has a monster crush on you."

"I know. Shall we?" He places a hand on the small of my back and guides me toward the gangway.

I ignore the heat from his big hand on my lower back and allow it to remain there as a test of my fortitude. I will courageously resist temptation with every ounce of mental and emotional strength within me. Also, his hand feels too good to push away.

I look up at him. "So you just encourage her crush on you when there's no chance?"

He shrugs one shoulder.

"What if she's turning down guys because she thinks she's in love with you?"

He drops his hand from my back and stares at me. "You think she's in love with me?"

"Why not? You're gorgeous, warm, and kind to her. Not to mention a frigging prince."

A slow smile breaks until he's smiling widely, his teeth flashing white against the dark stubble of his jaw. I am immune, dammit.

"What?" I ask.

"That might be the nicest thing anyone's ever said to me. The warm and kind part, not the frigging prince part."

I give him my best menacing scowl, though being a petite five-foot happy pixie, I can never quite pull it off. "Just don't break her heart. I like her."

"I do too, Ruby. I do too."

A stab of jealousy alarms me. Maybe Maya does have a chance with him.

And why do I care?

4

Phillip

I'm only here to help out Anna. When my sister-in-law returns from her honeymoon to my steadfast refusal to set foot in a bachelor auction, at least I can feel good about helping her friend with the royal fantasy suite. I tell myself that's more than enough. I will make myself useful to Ruby, and she will hopefully pass along how helpful I've been.

Except I know that's not the only reason I'm here. I want to spend more time with Ruby. Yesterday when I kept my distance after her open friendliness, I felt like I'd lost something important. She's beautiful and has such joie de vivre, an inner spark of enthusiasm, an energy I find irresistible. I can't deny the attraction, and I know it goes both ways. It's like a living, breathing thing between us. Would it be so bad if I acted on it?

Yes! It would be very bad. Anna already warned you off.

I pull out my phone. Look, there it is, Anna's Ruby-is-forbidden text. *We need her, and I can't afford to have you screw it up like you do with every other woman.*

And this little gem: *I love you, just keep it in your pants.*

I study our texts for a moment. You know, it doesn't say I can't be *friends* with Ruby. I will stand on that virtuous mountain until I die of unsatisfied lust. Or until Ruby goes back to the US next week. That's another good reason to keep it in my trousers. She's leaving; I'm leaving. She's not into casual sex, according to Anna, which means she'd regret a fling with me.

I'm not known for my steadfast commitment. Not since my ex, Lana. Our five-year relationship ended in a very public breakup that was well documented in the press and gossip rags. I admit I went a little nuts rutting my way through Europe after that. None of those women were right. I couldn't make the leap to a third date let alone commitment. And then I met Hailey, the wedding planner for my sister Silvia's wedding in the US. I purposely sabotaged myself by picking her to get closer to, a woman who was clearly in love with another man.

I exhale sharply. I've given up on finding the right woman. Maybe down the line I'll agree to an arranged marriage to benefit the kingdom. It was an option offered to me and my siblings, though only Gabriel and Emma agreed to it. Gabriel changed his mind when he met Anna. Emma is still engaged and seems content with the arrangement.

I look down from the captain's perch of the yacht, where I've been standing with the crew, at Ruby and Maya by the deck rail taking in the view as Villroy fades in the distance. They're a study in contrasts—the blond Ruby with her hair wild and loose in the sea breeze, the brunette Maya, her hair mostly still contained in a neat bun. Maya is dressed in her uniform of white shirt and black trousers, while Ruby is all color in a vibrant floral dress in shades of red, pink, and yellow. Maya is composed propriety, albeit with a sense of humor. Ruby is looser, more open.

I take in the island that is home. It's mostly untouched by modern times, though we do have cell phones and internet. The coastline is rugged with cliffs. Inlets with gorgeous sand beaches nestle between the cliffs. Port Axel is the main commercial base for fishermen, who mostly catch tuna, bass, monkfish, and shellfish. There's an old lighthouse with a red top, the locals' white boats anchored near the port, and farther out by the port are white buildings with red roofs for the commercial fishing industry. Inland and along the road to the palace are cottages, white with blue trim, and even farther out dunes and wetlands. Villroy is a part of me, and no matter how far away I travel, I always return home. I'm lucky enough to live in Amalie Palace, perched in the center of the island on a hill overlooking it all.

I join the women at the deck rail, standing next to Ruby. "Hello. Enjoying the view?"

She smooths her long dirty blond hair back behind her ears before turning to me. "Absolutely. The palace looks like something out of a fairy tale, even more so from a distance."

I smile. I've heard that before, but to me it's simply home. Amalie Palace is sandstone with copper roofs, five stories, reaching six stories in the two towers. There's two long wings stretching out from the sides that form a courtyard in back, leading to manicured gardens and a long path to the sea.

"I think the last renovation is what put it over the edge with all the spires," I tell her. "Fire took some of the earlier palaces. This one was built in the eighteenth century and renovated many times."

She turns back to the view. "It's enchanting."

"To think my Viking ancestors started with a plain stone circular fortress." I point over to the crumbling structure perched on one side of the palace.

"Is that what that is?" She turns to me and crinkles her nose. "I like the newer one better." Her hair flies into her face as the yacht angles into a turn, and she holds it down with both hands. "Isn't it a hazard to have a pile of rocks like that? It looks like it could crumble at any moment."

"It reminds us of our heritage, our history, and it reminds the islanders that the proper family is ruling. It was our ancestors who started the settlement."

"Cool." She lets go of her hair and it slaps her in the face. I barely resist smoothing it back for her. She spits some out and smooths it back. "I should've brought a hair band or a hat."

"We could go in the cabin." I gesture to the enclosed cabin behind us. "You can still have the view. There's a sofa, TV, wet bar, refrigerator."

She peers in one of the windows. "Sure." She turns to Maya. "You want to go inside with us?"

Maya smiles. "Thanks, but I'd like to enjoy the sun a bit, ma'am. You go ahead."

Ruby turns to me. "Okay, lead the way."

So I do, telling myself it's harmless. An hour together in an enclosed cabin. It's not like I'm taking her to the master bedroom suite. I open the door for her and follow her in.

She stops short. "This is gorgeous!"

"Thanks. Though I really shouldn't take the credit."

She moves farther into the cabin. "It's so sleek."

There's a white leather sectional, a glossy wood coffee table with matching cabinetry, and hardwood flooring. The ceiling is white with recessed lighting and glossy light wood trim that matches the furnishings and floor. Past the wet bar is a dining area on a raised platform with a bay of windows.

"I suppose it's sleek because it has to weather the sea," I say. "Please have a seat. Would you like a drink?"

She sits in the center of the sectional across from the TV. "Sure! What do you have?"

I head over to the nearby wet bar. "Anything. It's fully stocked."

Her brows lift. "Is it too early for a margarita?"

I grin. It's not yet noon. "Never. But I'm afraid I'm your bartender. I can pour scotch, whisky, beer, or wine. Not much of a cocktail maker."

"Wow, a prince is serving me? Has this ever happened in the long history of the kingdom?"

I jab a finger at her. "Just for that you're getting bilge water."

She sticks out her tongue. "That sounds bad."

"It is bad. It's the dirty water that collects in the bottom of the boat." I open the liquor cabinet and scan the contents. Fully stocked as usual, along with snacks—pretzels, roasted nuts, chips, dried fruit, and trail mix.

She appears at my side. "You weren't kidding on the fully stocked. Now I wish I wasn't so full from breakfast. You royals really know how to eat. Do you have iced tea?"

I head over to the refrigerator across the cabin. "We do." I hand her the glass bottle and take a bottled water for myself.

She peers over at the dining area. "Ooh, let's sit there. It's a nice view of where we're heading."

I follow her to the table, and she takes a seat, facing the view. I sit to her right and stealthily admire her admiring the view. She's so vibrant, her hair tousled from the wind, a light pink flush to her cheeks. My mind flashes to a bed-rumpled Ruby after a hard—no. Off-limits. Forbidden. I force myself to look out the window to the sea.

Silence stretches between us.

Suddenly I'm nervous like we're on a first date and the long silence means it's going terribly. I don't get nervous on real first dates, why should I now? My hands are clammy, and my throat is suddenly parched. I open my bottled water and take a long swallow, suddenly conscious of the sound of my swallowing.

She opens her iced tea with a loud pop as the seal is broken, and takes a sip.

Say something!

"So how do you know Anna?" I ask.

She smiles, and I immediately relax. "She was the super in our apartment building in Tampa. The woman can fix anything! I was there for about a month when my refrigerator stopped working. Not only did she fix it, she told me to help myself to her refrigerator while I waited. I mean, we barely even knew each other, and she's handing me the keys to her apartment so I won't be inconvenienced."

"That sounds like her. Generous and unconventional."

"Yes! Anyway, I stayed and chatted with her while she was working on my refrigerator, and we just hit it off. We had an impromptu party at her place to celebrate my refrigerator being back in business. She made crushed ice with a wooden mallet and a sack! Actually, we both took turns smashing that ice, and then she made us Moscow mules." She sighs. "I moved to Orlando for a job, but we still hung out. It's not too far from Tampa. I'm really going to miss her now that she lives here permanently. She's the real deal, you know?"

"We're lucky to have her. So you're here for a week, right? Or will you be staying longer to spend time with her?" I should've asked her that earlier. I assumed she'd leave when she'd finished her work on the suite.

"Two weeks. She arrives Sunday and I leave the following Sunday."

"I leave the day after you for a five-week international tour with Global Sun Water. They're a nonprofit that works to bring solar water pumps to impoverished countries. After that, I'll start my work travelling as the UN Ambassador for Clean Water."

She pauses, her iced tea halfway to her mouth. "I did not expect that. That's great that you're involved in such a worthy cause."

I stiffen. Clearly she thought I was shallow. "You expected me to fill my days shopping and skulking around the palace?"

She laughs. "So how does it work with the solar water pumps?"

I fill her in on the technology, which is really just smart engineering. It's hard to imagine life without such a basic resource readily at hand. For many villages, it's the first time they've had a constant nearby water supply.

"The technology makes it possible to move past survival mode," I conclude.

"And what's your part?"

"I'm the one that brings the spotlight to their cause. I travel with Global Sun Water to the villages, but I also meet with diplomats and leaders and cut a lot of red ribbons for the press." I've contributed generously to them as well, but I leave that out. I don't do it for recognition. I do it because I believe in the cause.

She shakes her head. "Phillip, you have unsuspected depth."

That stings, but I keep my tone light. "Not just a pretty face, huh?"

She slaps a hand over her mouth. "It did sound like that, didn't it? I'm sorry." She drops her hand. "I must've had some impression of what you were like, you know, from all the pictures of you gallivanting on the beach with supermodels."

"I do not gallivant." I crinkle my brow. "Or do I? Care to demonstrate a gallivant?"

She surprises me by standing and moving to the center of the cabin. I step down into the main cabin to get a better view.

"I imagine it's something like this." She grabs the end of her dress and swishes about the cabin before stopping, dipping an imaginary partner over her arm, and puckering up.

"Not quite."

"More like this?" She runs in slow motion toward me, her arms out as if to embrace me. She has a big exaggerated smile on her face like she's ecstatic to see me.

I match her big fake smile, opening my arms to her. She doesn't halt at the invitation, instead she closes the distance. I hug her and spin her around, pretending I'm ecstatic to see her.

Except with Ruby in my arms, her gaze searching mine, it suddenly feels very real.

~

Ruby

My heartbeat roars in my ears, my senses tilting at the unexpected dizzying pleasure of Phillip spinning me around. He stops spinning, still holding me around the waist, my feet dangling above the ground. We're eye to eye. He's taller than me, so I don't usually get this up-close view. I notice every detail, his dilated pupils, the dark blue ring around the iris, the thick lashes. A man should not be this beautiful.

His voice comes out rough. "I should put you down." He makes no move to release me.

I stare at his mouth, at his full lower lip that's been tempting me from the start. "Can I just..." I close the distance and dart my tongue out to taste.

He groans and then his mouth seals over mine. It's not rough, not too soft; it's perfect. Decadent. Lush. I'm drowning in sensation, in the pleasure of kissing this beautiful man. I can barely catch my breath and I don't care. I just need more. I'm suddenly ravenous for him, my long-dormant needs lurching back to life.

He breaks the kiss and sets me back on my feet. I'm not done. I wrap my arms around his neck, go up on tiptoe, and bite his full lower lip. He growls low in his throat, turning me and pinning me against the wall, his mouth devouring mine. I slide my fingers through his soft hair, loving the thickness, loving everything about this—his taste, his scent, the way he kisses me like he's as hungry for me as I am for him.

He breaks the kiss suddenly, turns toward the cabin door, and bites out, "What?"

Whoa. I didn't even hear it open.

It's Maya, her eyes wide as she takes in me plastered

between the wall and Phillip. She lets out a soft cry, whirls, and rushes out of the cabin.

He closes his eyes and lets out a heavy sigh. Somehow I know he's going to comfort her.

"Hasn't she seen you with a woman before?" I whisper.

He steps back and runs a hand through his hair. "Not quite that up close. I don't bring women home, except for my ex, and that was more than a year ago."

"Ah."

He smiles ruefully. "I know I should go talk to her, but I don't think it'll go over well while I'm in this state." He gestures below the waist at an impressive bulge.

A vision of Phillip's naked muscular body rising over me, covering me, driving into me flashes through my mind. I lift my head, my mouth dry. "Probably not."

He takes a deep breath. "I shouldn't have kissed you."

"It's fine."

He meets my eyes, his brows knitting together. "I don't know what came over me. We only have a couple of weeks before we go our separate ways. And I don't want hurt feelings, especially with a friend of my sister-in-law." He grimaces and looks away.

He's right. I wish he wasn't. I'm feeling things I haven't felt in a long time—warmth, affection, lust. He's not the arrogant jerk I first thought he was. I like him. And I don't kid myself that the incredible kiss we just shared would happen for me with any attractive guy. Usually, a first kiss is tentative, awkward, or sloppy. Sometimes all three. This was passionate perfection. That's rare and special and…impossible. We live in different worlds, soon to go our separate ways, and he's a renowned playboy. I know better than to get tangled up with him, no matter how tempting he is.

He looks so miserable I let him off the hook, saying nonchalantly, "No problem. We'll just rewind."

I open my arms and jog backward to the center of the cabin like I'm rewinding, running away from my lover through a meadow.

He grins and lifts his palms. "I'd like to say that worked, but…"

I head over to the sofa. "Come on, we'll watch some TV. You should probably talk to Maya once you two can have some privacy. I'm sure she won't appreciate your *it's not you, it's me* talk with me standing nearby."

He sits next to me and snags the remote from a compartment behind us. "I was going to go with 'we grew up together, so I've always seen you as a little sister.'"

I give him serious side-eye. "You can do better than that."

"How about 'I just don't feel that way about you'?"

"*Brraap*. Wrong answer."

He turns on the TV with a frown, rapidly flipping channels. "What should I say? I thought it was a harmless crush. Maya's mother worked as a maid for our family, and Maya started working for us when she was sixteen. I was nineteen. She really has felt like a little sister."

"Oh, wow. So the crush goes way back?"

"I suppose. She did blush a lot around me back then. Anyway, I'm twenty-nine. I thought she would've figured out by now it's not going to happen."

I wince. I suppose there isn't really a nice way to turn down an unrequited crush. "Go with the little-sister thing. She's going to be hurt no matter what you say. At least that's the gentlest of the nothing-personal responses."

He lands on a soccer game on the TV and puts the remote down. I pick it up, change the channel to a fashion show, and grin at him.

He holds me by the chin and kisses me, a swift hard kiss that jolts my system, leaving me speechless. Then he pulls out his phone, ignoring the TV.

Warmth steals through me. I know it's dumb. It's just a TV show, but my ex never let me have control of the remote. It's the little things. I can't help myself. I grab him and hug him tight around the middle. He smiles down at me, and it's like warm sunshine all over my body.

I let him go and get comfortable, scooching down in the cushy sofa and leaning against his side. His hand slides over and holds mine in a warm clasp.

My stupid heart flip-flops.

My lips curl up into a smile.

We are not done.

5

Ruby

Someone must've leaked the news about our arrival because when we step onto the dock in Nantes, there's a crowd of people waiting. Locals holding up their phones for pictures, but also what has to be paparazzi, their cameras with huge zoom lenses aimed at Phillip. They want the royal hottie.

Security flanks us. Phillip puts an arm around me, tucking me close to his side. A woman rushes toward us, screaming his name and knocking into Maya. Phillip grabs Maya and tucks her under his other arm. People are screaming "Prince Phillip" and "royal hottie," firing questions at him in English and French. I only catch a few things.

"Two women? Just one won't do it for you, huh, stud?"

"Who're the girls?"

"Lana's single again. Give her a call and you've got an orgy!" A ripple of laughter goes through the crowd.

I cringe. That's his ex. Their relationship was very

public. The press dubbed them "the golden couple." I would've hated that kind of scrutiny on my private relationship. The gossip rags covered the breakup and Lana's new lover in excruciating detail.

Phillip doesn't react, his expression neutral as he guides us through the crowd, the guards clearing a path. We're hustled into a waiting limo, and Phillip urges me and Maya in first. I hurry to the far side, making room for them. Maya takes the seat adjacent to me, clasping her hands tightly in her lap. The moment the door shuts behind Phillip, the car takes off.

Phillip sits on the bench seat next to me and leans toward Maya. "Are you okay?"

She looks down at her hands. "Yes, sir, I'm fine."

He turns to me in question.

"I'm fine."

He leans back and blows out a breath. "Shit. They'll make a story out of this, something as simple as a shopping trip. It's ridiculous. Why can't they just report on real news? Something worthwhile!"

"Your trip with Global Sun Water should help," I offer.

His eyes flash. "That's what they should be focused on. Clean water, helping people. Not my social life. Who cares?"

I lift one shoulder. "I don't."

He laughs. "All right. Enough agitating. Let's just enjoy ourselves." He glances over at Maya, who's quiet, still staring at her hands.

I tip my head toward the center console, where champagne is cooling in an ice bucket.

"Maybe we should start our trip with a little champagne," he announces. "Sound good, ladies?"

"Absolutely," I say.

"Maya?"

"I'm working, sir."

He lifts the champagne bottle. "You're officially off the clock. And if you want to wear something besides your uniform, you can pick an outfit at the shops. My gift to you."

Her head jerks up in surprise. "Really?"

"Yes, really. I've always thought of you as part of the family, like the agreeable little sister I never had." He cups his hand by his mouth and whispers conspiratorially, "Don't tell Emma and Silvia I said that." Those are his younger sisters.

She bites her bottom lip, fighting a smile. "Thank you, sir."

He pops the champagne, and Maya laughs at the sound. Just like that, Phillip has won her back to the friend side. He pours her a glass and hands it over; then he pours mine.

He offers me the glass with a wink. "For a supremely gifted gallivanter."

I flush at the memory of our shared gallivanting kiss. "Why, thank you." I take a sip and catch Maya's frown before she turns to look out the window.

Phillip

Other than the initial commotion at the dock, the rest of our trip runs smoothly. The palace staff is like a well-oiled machine when it comes to our outings. The shop-keepers are notified of our presence, and each store will close to customers during our visit with them. They're willing to do this because they know I have funds and any item I buy will instantly become popular. The fact that it's a Tuesday in September also makes it easier. We're not asking them to give up their busy weekend traffic.

We begin at le Passage Pommeraye because Maya is eager to find a new outfit and Ruby wants to see a historic shopping mall. They've cleared it for our private shopping trip for two hours. The moment we step inside, Ruby is enthralled. What was initially a passage between two streets is now a glass-covered, elaborately decorated three-story gallery of shops with a grand central staircase.

"Oh, look at these columns!" Ruby exclaims, pulling her phone out of her purse and snapping pictures. "And the arch, the clock, the cherubs!" She points at the carved cherubs overlooking the passage. "Aren't they darling? Even the windows are gorgeous!"

It is charming, a very typical French neoclassical style. The enclosed shops used to be outdoors, so they have their original windows with intricately carved plaster trim and wrought-iron flower boxes under the sill. The arch of the passageway features more fancy trim and a large clock. The glass ceiling lets in muted natural light.

I turn to Ruby. "Are you just going to keep taking pictures, or are we going to shop?"

She stashes her phone in her purse. "You and Maya hit the clothing shops. I'm going to check out some of these quirky-looking places. This place is magic!"

I leave her to it.

An hour later, Ruby is still off shopping somewhere, and Maya has emerged with her new outfit—a rust-colored blazer over a matching T-shirt with black trousers and black leather high-heeled boots. She's let her hair out of its bun, and the transformation is startling. She doesn't look like the Maya I grew up with. She looks like a stylish young woman, sexy even, with her dark brown hair falling in soft waves over her shoulders.

"Maya, you look lovely. You should get away from the palace, meet people your age, and socialize more." She rarely takes time off.

"Thank you, sir." Her cheeks flush pink. "Where would you have me go?"

"Wherever the cool guys your age go. Maybe here or Paris."

She tucks her hands behind her back. "Paris is a long train trip."

I realize my easy access to the yacht and jet have made me take my freedom for granted. "Well, then, on Villroy."

"There's not that many young men left there; only a few have joined their fathers in the fishing trade." She's probably known them her whole life and hasn't felt strongly about any of them. I suddenly want more for her than an unrequited crush on me. I want her to get out there and grab her own happiness. I never gave much thought to how insular life was for her. She's young. She should be out partying, dating the wrong guys, and having fun while doing it.

I rub my stubbled jaw. "Well, that is a problem. I think that will turn around once the queen's ideas get off the ground with the day spa and natural beauty product line. We'll likely have an influx of young people and visitors."

She murmurs noncommittally, seeming unconvinced.

"Maybe one of my brothers can introduce you to a friend or—"

Her cheeks flush scarlet. "Please don't trouble yourself finding me a date, sir."

I shut my mouth. I've never spent time with Maya outside the palace walls, and it reminds me of my privilege. I must remember gratitude and continue my efforts to give to others. That's the only meaningful use of what I've been given. Maybe Lana did me a favor by dumping me. I was at such loose ends I threw myself into distractions—women, yes, but also filling my schedule with charity events and going anywhere they wanted royal representation. Gabriel was still shunning the spotlight at the time. I'd long been a contributor to Global Sun Water, but it was a face-to-face meeting with the director at a fundraiser that led to my more active involvement.

"Phillip! Maya! Look at these treasures!"

I look up to the second floor, already smiling, where Ruby stands overshadowed by two carved Grecian columns with finials. Two burly shopkeepers hold the columns upright.

Ruby calls down to us. "These weren't even for sale! They were decorations. Aren't they amazing?"

Maya nods and smiles.

The columns look fake. I imagine they're chipped wood. "Wow." It's all I can come up with.

The men head for the grand staircase with the columns, and Ruby trots ahead of them. When she reaches us, she tells us in a low voice, "They were a steal! I'm going to sand them down and do this paint finish that will make them look less Grecian and more royal fantasy suite."

I have no idea what she means, but she's glowing with enthusiasm, her green eyes sparkling, her cheeks flushed pink, and I can do nothing but agree. "Wonderful choice."

"Thank you." She turns to Maya and does a comical double take. "Holy foxiness, woman! I almost didn't recognize you in that outfit and with your hair down. You are one hot mama!"

Maya smooths her hair, her cheeks flaming. "Thank you, ma'am."

Ruby smiles. "I know guys who would trip over their own tongues just trying to ask you out." She turns to me. "Right?"

"Yes, she looks lovely. Would you like an outfit too?"

"Me? Oh, no. I've got limited time to get the suite ready, and I need to be efficient." She hurries over to the men with the columns, giving them directions. They look confused.

I head over and direct them in French to put the columns on the yacht, where the crew will help get them on board. Then I call ahead to give the crew advance warning. By the time I finish, Ruby is looking at me like she's about to leap into my arms and kiss me senseless. There's no other description for the adoring lustful look in her eyes.

She goes up on tiptoe and whispers in my ear, "You sound so sexy speaking in French."

I grin because giving directions isn't sexy. I whisper in her ear in French that I enjoy the library. It was one of the first phrases I was taught by my French tutor.

Her eyes glow at me adoringly, her voice breathy. "That is hot."

And now I know the key to seducing Ruby. Guilt stabs at me and I look away. Anna warned me off Ruby and she's right. I'm not looking for serious, Ruby doesn't do casual, and we're heading our separate ways soon. That means I need to shift back to the friend zone no matter how much lust glows in her eyes. Or grows in my trousers.

I force my mind away from its usual lusty path and focus on the fact that Anna would kill me for hooking up with Ruby. Gabriel would likely join the fray, always taking her side. You don't piss off the king and queen.

Ruby

This week has been a whirlwind. I've been so laser-focused on pulling the fantasy suite together before Anna arrives, I've barely stopped to eat. I put in long hours, along with Maya and Phillip, and I'm proud of the way it has come together. It's now Sunday morning, the guests arrive tonight, and Anna is due any moment.

I take a final walk-through of the master suite and then stop by the adjoining rooms. My only regret is that I didn't have time to order what would've been a fantastic regal touch—stained-glass windows with the royal crest. It's unnecessary, really, with the view of the island and the sea from here, but there's something so special about the glow of light through stained glass. Maybe I'll suggest light boxes behind stained glass as a future add-on.

I've already taken pictures both with my phone and my digital camera for my portfolio. In addition to the antique mahogany furniture, I've installed golden sconces throughout the space that look like candles but are really lights. The antique tabletop clock and vintage phone previously taken from the attic are now in the master living room and bedroom respectively. The Grecian columns were color washed with satin and metallic paint to make a glowing light gold, and set in the master bedroom. Each column is topped with a cherub I found in an antique shop in Nantes. The gold color continues on the decorative pillows and throw blankets on the beds and sofas.

The ceiling paintings turned out amazing! Even better than I imagined. The master living room's fantasy seascape painting is trimmed in a curving gold frame. Clara really captured the blue-green of the sea here, which is the gorgeous backdrop for mermaids and nymphs, along with dolphins, fish, and seabirds. The starry sky paintings over the tubs in each bathroom are dreamy, and the acoustic panels help create a warm hushed sound. Phillip took care of restoring the fireplace mantel himself. He surprised me with his offer to help. I gave him some instruction on stripping the old paint, sanding, and painting. Jeanne then carefully replicated the original royal crest at the center of the mantel and added a thin line of gold paint along the top of it on the crown's edges.

The suite of rooms says elegance and grand royal tradition. I love it so much I want to move in. I take a seat in front of the new fireplace mantel in the master suite's living room to wait for Anna. I'm not sure how many women were invited for the ladies' week, but the suite, along with the adjoining rooms, can sleep eight, if the women don't mind sharing a bed. Each room has a king-sized bed. No sleeper sofas. Maybe that was on purpose to limit the number of guests. The palace is still a private residence.

"Ruby! Ahhh! Get over here!"

I turn at the sound of Anna's voice, and she looks happier than I can ever remember seeing her. Her wild dark curls frame a heart-shaped face flushed pink with excitement, her brown eyes sparkling, her smile beaming. She's wearing a form-fitting black long-sleeved dress that ends mid-thigh with leopard-print heels. Still the Anna I know. She's always had a thing for leopard prints. She says the leopard is her spirit animal.

I rush to hug her, and she envelops me in a monster hug, crushing me against her chest. She's taller than me, like most people.

She pulls back and holds me by the shoulders. "It's so good to see you! Thank you so much for coming to our rescue!"

That's Anna for you. This was practically an act of charity on her part. She already had a gorgeous suite and was generous enough to offer me work to add my own personal touch. This is a fabulous prestigious project to add to my portfolio. "Thank you for the opportunity. Really. I owe you big time. And I'm so sorry I couldn't make it to your wedding. It was at the same time as my parents' twenty-fifth anniversary party, which I planned." She knows I'm their only child, so she understood. Though soon I'll have a little sister! Only four months until she's due.

"I know. I missed you, but it's okay."

"Honestly, even if it wasn't their anniversary, I didn't have the funds to travel out here, and I would've been too embarrassed to ask you to cover me. Before I started this job, I was at a real low point. Broke, unemployed, living with my parents, nursing a broken heart from a man who basically lied to me the entire year we were together. Married with triplets on the way sent me in a tailspin."

She shakes her head. "He sucks! You deserve so much better."

"Thanks. Again, I'm sorry I missed your wedding—"

"Stop, girl. Nothing to be sorry about. I understood you had other priorities, and I totally get being in a tough place and feeling like there's no way out. Now let me see what you did here." She does a slow turn, taking in the master living room.

I hold my breath. I so want to please her. She's done so much for me, giving me this project.

"Oh, wow," she breathes. "This is exactly what it needed. That extra layer of sparkle. It feels extra royal now."

"Phillip helped restore the mantel. It was in the attic."

She raises her brows. "Phillip knows how to restore a mantel?"

"I taught him. He's been really helpful."

"Really?" She drawls the word out almost like she's suspicious.

I nod.

"Hmm…" She looks up at the ceiling and squeaks. "Ruby! This is incredible! Who did this?"

"Maya and I tracked down two artists on the island. Clara did the sea painting, and Jeanne did the starry skies over the whirlpool tubs. The tub paintings are made from acoustic panel so it muffles the echo and also doubles as a pretend skylight."

"Get. Out." She rushes to the master bathroom. "I love it! I never would've thought of this." She turns to me. "Ruby, you're a genius! I can't believe you haven't been inundated with new work now that you're freelance."

I shift on the balls of my feet, torn between pride in my work and shame for not getting my new freelance career off the ground. Some part of me blames my lingering gloom, preventing me from getting that crucial word-of-mouth going. "It's tough to get some momentum in the beginning. I've had a few small jobs. I'm hoping adding this project to my portfolio will give me a boost."

She wanders into the master bedroom and runs her fingers along the gold silk throw pillows and the soft gold throw. "It feels extra royal with all the touches of gold.

And these columns! I love it!" She picks up the antique phone on an end table. "Does this thing work?"

"It's decorative. I think it needs to be rewired."

"I'll do it today." I immediately picture her whipping out her tool belt. It's cool that she's so handy, but I know she has royal duties to attend to now.

"It doesn't have to work. Maybe your guests would like to unplug. You know, like they're temporarily living in a retro, less hectic time."

"Good point." She heads to the door to the adjoining suite, a smaller version of this one, checking everything out.

I follow her through all the rooms as she *oohs* and *aahs*.

"How was your honeymoon?" I ask when she's finally done exclaiming over my genius. She's really much too generous with her praise. On the other hand, if every client was like this, I would be one happy camper.

"Fabulous." She takes a seat on the bed in one of the smaller bedrooms. "I learned so much." Not what I expected her to say.

I sit next to her and grin. "You learned so much on your honeymoon? Your husband must be very skilled."

We crack up.

"He's amazing, of course," she says. "But I was also soaking in the women's style in Paris, Milan, and Barcelona." She lowers her voice conspiratorially. "Kind of a research trip slash honeymoon. Don't tell Gabriel."

"Like I would rat you out to the king."

She laughs. "So did you meet everyone? Oscar, Lucas, Adrian, and Emma? I'm told my mother-in-law hasn't left her rooms."

"Adrian was away, but yes to everyone else. Phillip introduced me when they each stopped by to see what he was so busy doing in here. Everyone's been very warm and gracious."

She purses her lips. "How's Phillip been treating you?"

My cheeks flush. "Good."

She nods once, her curls bouncing. "Good. I told him to keep it in his pants."

"Anna!"

"What? I know he's a player, you've been through hell with your asshole ex, and you've never been a casual-fling kind of woman." She gives my arm a squeeze. "Plus, you're getting your new business off the ground. You don't need any distractions right now."

My shoulders droop. "True." Why do I feel let down? She's right. Besides, Phillip and I only kissed once. Mostly we've been working since I had such a tight deadline to get the suite ready. Some small part of me must've been hoping for a little more. The chemistry sizzles between us just from standing near each other.

"Why do you sound so sad?" she asks. "Did you want to hook up with Phillip?"

I square my shoulders. "No, of course not."

"He is hot."

"Undeniably."

"He's also a manwhore." She shrugs. "I love him, but he is. I recommend you keep him at arm's length."

"What about Lana? He was with her for years. Maybe deep down he's hoping to meet the right woman."

She grabs me by the shoulders and turns me toward her. "Ruby, listen to me, do *not* think you can fix him or magically be the one to make him commit. I know he can be charming, but don't open yourself up to what will only hurt you. I say this because I love you."

"I know." I swallow my disappointment. He grew on

me, I guess. "It's not going to be an issue. We're both leaving next week. He's going on a charitable tour for a really long time. Could be a year or more with his work for the UN, and I'm going back home to patch together enough work to move out of my parents' house. Not just because I want to launch my business. My mom is five months pregnant and they need my room."

Her hand flies to her mouth. "Oh my God! How old is she?"

"Forty-three. It's her miracle baby. We're all so excited."

"Congratulations! I know how much you've always wanted a sibling."

I nod. I can't manage words with the lump in my throat. There's so much I want to do with my little sister, so much I want to teach her and show her.

She taps a scarlet fingernail with rhinestones against her red-painted lips. "I bet when my guests see what you did with this suite, they'll want to hire you. They're all very successful in their fields and own their own homes. Plus, they're local for you, from the Tampa area. Sixteen women with plenty of cash to burn. I'll introduce you as the interior designer as soon as they arrive."

A surge of excitement has me grabbing her in a hug. "That would be amazing!"

She laughs. "I am pretty amazing."

I let her go, smiling so big my cheeks hurt. If these well-to-do women like my work, not only would I have a fabulous start, but I'd finally get the word-of-mouth I need for my career to take off. It would mean so much at this point in my life to prove I can be a success.

I hug her again. "Thank you, thank you, thank you!"

"There's the happy Ruby I remember, and you're quite

welcome. Honestly, your work speaks for itself." She gestures around the room.

I look around with a critical eye, but even picky me is pleased with the results. Sixteen potential new clients, wow. Wait a minute. "Sixteen guests? Anna, where will they sleep? There's only beds for half that."

She winces. "I know, it was originally eight, but when word leaked out about the royal bachelor auction, more of my clients begged me for an invite. I couldn't turn them down."

I still. "Say what? Royal bachelor auction?"

"Phillip didn't tell you?"

"No."

"He's the headliner. Plus his younger single brothers. You should bid on Adrian. He's the only one I'd trust not to seduce you. He's too much of a gentleman."

I crinkle my nose. "First, I'm broke, and second, *eww.* I'm not going to bid on a man like some kind of weird trophy." It hits me then. That must be why Phillip told me he wouldn't go on a date with me for any price when I first arrived at the palace. He must've thought I was one of Anna's clients eager for the royal bachelor auction. Now why didn't he just explain that? I totally would've understood. Poor guy must've felt like he *had* to do this embarrassing auction for Anna. No wonder he seemed so agitated the first time we met.

Anna goes on. "It's not like a man trophy. See, it's a fundraiser for the next phase of my plan, the day spa. I want them to feel invested in it so they'll return and spread the word about how amazing it is. The women can bid on winning a date with a prince, just a date, I was clear on that. Anyway, it's Phillip and his single brothers in the auction, but Phillip is the big draw. He's famous as the royal hottie. My clients are beside themselves over who's going to win a date with him."

I press my lips together, ignoring the burn of jealousy in my chest. Phillip is not mine.

"Would you mind being the designated bid starter?" she asks. "Adrian is first up. Fifty euros is the opening bid."

Everyone wants Phillip. He's a world-famous playboy prince. I have to remember that, no matter how down-to-earth and friendly he seemed this past week. He belongs to the world of glamorous wealthy women. And that is not me. Besides, I know better than to cross the line for a fling with no future. The last thing I want is to leave here nursing a broken heart. Been there, got the hideous T-shirt.

Will he hook up with one of Anna's wealthy clients? My gut churns.

"Ruby?"

My head jerks up. "Yeah?"

"Lost you there for a minute. Would you mind being the bid starter for Adrian? Fifty euros."

"Sure." I figure her clients will quickly outbid me, so the money isn't a concern.

"Great! We're having a cocktail hour before, and then I've got more food, drinks, and a DJ for the big event with dancing after. It'll be one big blowout party."

I paste on a smile. "I'll be there." I'm up for a party. Watching women drool over Phillip while he flirts, not so much. I hate that I care.

She stands. "I'd better go check on the guest rooms on the third floor. The original eight I invited will get this suite. I didn't want you to fancy up the other rooms because we really are trying to limit the number of visitors going forward. Of course, all of them will get their hair, facial, and nails done by me. Beauty treatments are part of the package. Gabriel says I shouldn't be doing that now that I'm queen, royal protocol yada yada yada. I say I can do what I want in the privacy of our home."

I stand too. "Sounds wonderful. When's the auction?"

"Tomorrow night. Oh, and I got the cutest G-strings for them to wear under—" she grabs at imaginary pant legs "—strippable pants."

I instantly imagine Phillip in a striptease, the women clawing their way to him. "My God."

"I'm joking!" She gives my arm a squeeze. "Relax, it'll be fun!"

6

―――――

Phillip

"Look who showed up," Lucas drawls. "Mr. I'm Above All This."

"Shut it," I snap at my younger brother. We're standing backstage for the royal bachelor auction. So how did I get here, headlining the bachelor auction I was so staunchly against? One word—Ruby. Anna too. Okay, two words.

"Ruby will be at the auction," Anna said this morning at breakfast when I told her to make her guests stop hounding me. Last night one of them actually ripped the rear pocket off my trousers to take home as a souvenir! If security hadn't closed in, I'm sure my shirt would've been ripped off as well!

"Mmm-hmm." I keep a neutral expression as Anna watches me like a hawk across the table. It's just the two of us in the parlor for a late breakfast. I'm not sure if Ruby shared with Anna that we kissed. Ruby and I have done an admirable job pretending that kiss never happened. The electric attraction is harder to ignore. I've kept my hands to myself, and she's done her part by not running into my arms. I bite back a smile at the memory of her "gallivanting."

"She plans to bid on Adrian." Anna puts a hand to her heart. "It's so sweet of her to help out with my cause, even though she's broke. She can only afford the fifty-euro starting bid."

Adrian? He just arrived this morning from Monte Carlo. Ruby meets him once and spends her last euro on him while I suffer splinters and blisters helping her out all week? That ancient fireplace mantel and the chipped-wood columns didn't fix themselves up!

Anna takes a sip of tea before smiling sweetly. "I so, so appreciate you doing this auction. Not only to get my clients jazzed about the project, but with the money we raise, I hope to fund survey and engineering for the day spa and get some architectural drawings done, which, of course, I'll share with my clients. Then it's on to research and development for the beauty product line."

I'm both irritated that she assumes I'll do the auction after I very clearly refused, and insanely jealous that Ruby wants Adrian. I never get jealous. This is stupid. I know Ruby won't win the bid on him since she's broke. Yet it seems urgent that I'm there to make sure she doesn't do something, *anything* with Adrian. It's not just the auction. Afterward, there's a big party with a DJ, dancing, and plenty of alcohol. I can see that picture all too clearly— Ruby dancing with Adrian, Ruby grinding with Adrian, Ruby drunk, laughing, following him upstairs. No, she's not like that. But if she's tempted by Adrian after just meeting him, there's no telling what could happen. There will definitely be touching.

I take a ferocious bite of toast and chew.

Anna digs into her omelet, seeming oblivious to my agitation.

Irrational jealousy finally wins out, and I find myself saying, "Fine, I'll be there, but I'll be contributing as an anonymous donor to bid on myself."

Her brows scrunch together in confusion, her fork poised in midair. "You're going on a date with yourself?"

"With a woman of my choosing." Ruby. She'd never see me as an object, something to get a piece of and take home as a souvenir. She'd never brag she was with the royal hottie either because she sees me, Phillip Rourke, the man who works with his hands on fireplace mantels, speaks sexy French, and contributes to clean water efforts. "If I'm going to do this, it has to be under my control."

She sets her fork down and smiles tightly. "Did you have someone in mind?"

"I'll decide when the moment comes. Not the man-hungry woman who ripped my trousers, that's for sure." I go back to eating.

She tilts her head, studying me. "Kind of defeats the purpose of the auction if it's rigged."

"I don't see why. Your friends can still meet me, scream their heads off, whatever they want as long as they keep their hands to themselves. They just can't be alone with me."

"One of them will be alone with you on your date." She narrows her eyes. "It's Ruby, isn't it? She told me you helped her this past week working on the fantasy suite. Since when do you do manual labor?"

"I have many talents." A stretch. Ruby taught me what to do. "Ruby and I are friends. The date would be completely platonic."

"*Phillip.*"

She doubts my intentions, probably with good reason, but my need to prevent the Ruby-Adrian connection outweighs all other risks. I straighten my spine and say in my most imperious voice, "Anna, take it or leave it."

She caved. Her friends want to see me in the auction too much for Anna to disappoint them. I caved too, but it's on my terms and for a good reason.

So here I am in the ballroom, standing behind a red velvet curtain with my younger brothers. There's a small stage and a catwalk that leads down the center of the rows of chairs, where Anna's nutso wild friends will be sitting. I'm wearing one of my club outfits—black button-down shirt open at the collar, black leather trousers, and black motorcycle boots.

Lucas hip-checks me. My younger brother by a year resembles me with the same dark brown hair and blue-green eyes, though his beard hides the similar sharp lines of our cheekbones and jaw. "I bet I go for more than you."

I snort. I'm the headliner here.

"I want in if we're betting," Oscar says, joining us. "I bet Lucas goes for more than Phillip, and I go for more than both of you." He's three years younger than me at twenty-six, with the same coloring, but, by some fluke of nature, inherited a combination of our parents' traits that made him turn out the best looking of us. His face has perfect symmetry like you see on male models and movie stars. If he wasn't so discreet, he would probably be the one dubbed the royal hottie.

"I'm putting a hundred on Phillip," Adrian says, slapping a hand on my shoulder. Now that I've neutralized Adrian's possible claim on Ruby, I can enjoy his support. He's my youngest brother at twenty-three, same thick dark hair, but his eyes are hazel like our mother's.

"Thank you," I tell Adrian. He's a card shark and loves a good high-stakes poker game, but he's smart about his betting. He must really think I'm going to be the highest bid.

"Why's that?" Lucas asks Adrian.

Adrian lifts his palms. "He's the royal hottie. Anna's friends are mostly here for him."

Lucas shoots me a sideways look. "Maybe I'll put on a better show."

Oscar rubs his scruffy jaw. "Just because we're not an internet meme doesn't mean we can't outbid him. So how much do you want to wager?"

I ignore them as they whisper and shake hands, striking deals for the bets. I already know I'll win. I'm bidding on myself, and the women are crazy enough for me they'll surely keep up with my bids.

Women's laughter bursts through the room. Sixteen man-hungry women who all want a piece of me. The hair on the back of my neck rises as a horrifying image flashes through my mind—me flat on my back on the ground, the women ripping my clothes and yanking out locks of my hair. I'm having second thoughts. And third and fourth.

"They're here," Lucas says, rubbing his hands together. "This is going to be fun."

Fun? No. Torture is more like it. And, after the auction, the torture continues. Since there's only four princes up for auction, that means a lot of the women will be disappointed, so Anna asked us to spend time with them, mingling and dancing.

Anna bursts through the center of the red velvet curtains separating us from the stage, which exposes us to the women's view. They go wild with hoots and hollers. I do a quick scan of the crowd for Ruby before stepping out of view. I didn't see her. Lucas and Oscar are pointing at different women like they're picking them out personally. Adrian blows them a kiss.

"Royal hottie, you are mine!" the insane woman who took my trousers' pocket hollers.

"He's mine!" another woman hollers.

"I've already named our children!" someone hollers, and the women scream with laughter.

What if Ruby's a no-show?

Anna looks over her shoulder at her guests. "Bar's open, ladies! Help yourselves!"

"Woo-hoo!"

"Party!"

"Yeah! This place is the best!"

Great. Let's lower their inhibitions even more.

Anna closes the curtain behind her and says under her breath, "They're already wasted from the cocktail hour we just had. I didn't want them to feel too intimidated to bid on princes who date models."

My brothers smirk. I'm too busy thinking about an escape route.

Anna tosses her dark curls over her shoulder. She's wearing a tight sleeveless red dress with black stilettos. Much more revealing than what our queen would normally wear, but her husband, the king, allows it because he's crazy for her. "How're you guys doing? You feeling good?"

"Great!" my brothers assure her in near unison.

She turns to me. "Can't wait to see how high your bidding goes. The women are psyched. You'll be going on last to build the anticipation."

I nod once and work for a pleasant expression despite

the grim fortitude I'm drawing on to see this through. *Please let Ruby show up.*

"We'll get the bidding sky-high for you, Anna," Lucas says.

Oscar leans in, speaking in a low voice. "We've got a pool going."

"Phillip will crush it," Adrian says.

"I like your spirit!" Anna exclaims, beaming at us. Then she hugs each of us in turn and kisses our cheeks. "I love you, guys. You're the big brothers I always wished I had, except you, Adrian, since we're the same age. You could be my twin or triplet, I guess, since you already have Silvia for your twin. Anyhoo, break a leg!"

My brothers smile and nod. I try not to dwell on being ripped to bits by a hungry mob.

"Is Gabriel coming?" Lucas asks Anna casually, and I know exactly why. He's considering how outrageous he can be to win the betting pool.

"Of course!" Anna exclaims. "We're a team. He's with your mom right now, explaining why this auction is such a great idea. I guess I forgot to mention it."

Su-u-ure, forgot. Just like she forgot to mention the auction to me until the last minute. She's devious, that woman. But I have to admit, very effective.

She rushes through the curtains and calls to her friends, "Who's ready to party?"

The women cheer enthusiastically. Music blasts out of speakers near both sides of the stage, a low thumping bass beat. Oscar and Lucas start moving to the beat, getting some pelvic thrusts into it. Adrian takes one look at the horror on my face and cracks up.

It occurs to me with a jolt that Anna may have used Ruby's name to lure me here because she knows we've become friendly. She could've made up that bit about Ruby bidding on Adrian. Have I been outmaneuvered?

Hell, I may actually go to one of the wild mob.

~

Ruby

These ladies are so fun! I feel like I joined a raging party, even before the alcohol started flowing. I'm so glad I was invited to stay this extra week to hang with Anna. Not only has it given me time to reconnect with her and finally meet her husband, but I've gotten to meet her friends too. Anna took me with them on the tour of the royal fantasy suite and sang my praises. All of them wanted my number and swore they wanted me to take a look at their place the moment I get back home. I nearly cried. Sixteen potential clients in one fell swoop. What seemed like a lost cause suddenly feels like a real chance at a career. And it's all me—an entrepreneur—proving myself. It goes a long way after feeling like a failure. I was at a real low point before this trip, wallowing at home with nothing great on the horizon. Now everything feels bright, like the sun finally came out after a long stream of rainy days. I'm even starting to feel like my old energetic self again.

Actually, I started feeling more like my old self again the moment I got here. Maybe the tight deadline forced me to focus on work and freed my mind from dark thoughts of the past. Maybe it's Phillip. Despite his player rep, which frankly is a huge turnoff, he's grown on me. All of my nerves light up the moment he gets near. Who am I kidding? I'm hot for him.

"Can we switch seats?" Ashley, a woman with honey

blond hair, asks, leaning close. I can smell the alcohol on her breath. She's a corporate lawyer. I've memorized as many details as I could on my potential new clients. "I wanna be close enough to reach out and touch someone." She giggles.

I gape at her. "Um, I don't think we're supposed to touch."

She laughs. "Maybe they'll touch me. I could flash them." She goes to lift her blouse in demonstration, and I put my hand over hers, keeping it down.

I think of Phillip on display up there and can't help my indignation. "It's an auction for a date, *that's all.*"

"Geez, loosen up!" She tosses her hair, stands, and works her way around to the other side of the catwalk, sitting on the end over there.

Damn, I might've just lost her as a potential client. That worry is trounced by my indignation on Phillip and his brothers' behalf. The men are doing this as a fundraiser, and they shouldn't have to worry about grabbing hands. I know Phillip wouldn't like that. He carries himself with a certain princely dignity. I'm not sure about his brothers. Lucas and Oscar are pretty flirty. Of course, there is security. Twelve guards total, two per royal for the four princes, the king, and the queen. Anna confided to me that they didn't really need this much security for a closed palace event, but when the guards heard what she planned, they *wanted* to be here. Purely for their own amusement. *Men.*

Gradually, the women take their seats. Everyone has a drink in hand. I'm in the last row, still nursing the same glass of sauvignon blanc from the cocktail party earlier. I'm pacing myself since I'm such a lightweight. There's servants circulating to replenish drinks too.

The doors to the ballroom open and a servant announces, "King Gabriel and Queen Anna."

A hush falls over the room. Something about having them announced hits me with the importance of Anna's new role. I saw her earlier and she was just my friend Anna from Tampa. She left the ballroom a short while ago to go smooth things over with her mother-in-law, who's much more proper than Anna and apparently not happy about the auction.

Anna waves and smiles at everyone. Gabriel remains stone-faced, his posture stiff and proud, wearing a charcoal gray suit, no tie. I suppose that's casual for him. He places a hand on the small of her back and escorts her to the front podium on stage, where she will be announcing the auction. She turns to him, goes up on tiptoe, and gives him a peck on the lips. He's smiling when he takes his front-row seat and looks much warmer than when I met him earlier. I guess Anna has that effect on him.

Anna gestures to the DJ at the side of the room to turn down the music, and picks up a wireless microphone. "Can you hear me okay?"

"Yeah!" we all cheer. Some of the women wolf-whistle.

"All right! Let's get this thing started!" Anna gestures to a servant, who dims the lights. "First bachelor prince up for auction is Adrian Rourke. Let's give it up for this hottie!"

Adrian steps through the curtains and lifts a hand to us. He's wearing a white button-down shirt with black jeans and black high-top sneakers.

Anna gives us his highlights while he struts down the catwalk. I can only hear snippets of it because the women are screaming his name.

"Six feet of…"

"Has a girl twin, so he gets women…"

"Top honors at university…"

"Enjoys poker, including strip poker…"

The women go wild! The rest of his bio is drowned out, and Anna finally gives up. He's got a cocky grin on his face, looking pretty comfortable with the attention. He turns, makes his way back down the catwalk to center stage, and nods at Anna.

"Should we start the bidding?" she asks.

Adrian lifts his arms, waving us on. The noise is deafening—screaming, whistling, stamping feet.

"Bidding starts at fifty euros!" Anna hollers above the noise.

I raise my hand. "Fifty!" My one and only bid for the night. I agreed to be the designated person to get the ball rolling on bidding.

Anna beams at me. "We have fifty!"

"A thousand!" someone hollers.

"Two thousand!"

It keeps going, crazy high. Wow, this is going to be a killer fundraiser. Just wait until they get to the last prince, the royal hottie. The women will be frothing at the mouth. I cringe to think of Phillip on a date with one of these women. I have no right to be possessive of him, but, after getting to know him this week, I've seen glimpses of a tender side. He doesn't want to be mauled by an aggressive woman.

The bidding slows around five thousand euros, and Anna crosses to Adrian's side, goading them on. "Come on, ladies! This is a prince who's got it all. He's smart, he's good lookin', and he's a good dancer!"

The DJ cranks the music to a sexy hard beat, and Adrian and Anna start dancing together. It is *hot.* The pair of them move sensuously, close but not touching, Adrian smoldering down at her. Gabriel barks something from his seat, and Anna turns, makes a kissy face at him, and then hollers, "Go, Adrian!" She takes her place back at the podium.

He dances alone, lifting his arms and rolling his hips in a suggestive way. Then he moves forward, making eye contact with a woman in the front row, slowly raising the end of his shirt to reveal ripped abs. Damn, he is fine. They must have a personal trainer on staff at the palace. Phillip is similarly ripped.

The woman he aimed his abs at leaps out of her seat. "Six thousand!"

Adrian drops his shirt and does another walk down the catwalk. The bidding is insane. Ashley—the eager groper—lunges to grab Adrian's calf. Security instantly moves forward, but Adrian shakes his head at them. He drops to his haunches in front of her, takes her hand, and kisses the back of it. He whispers something to her, and she smiles and settles back in her seat.

Then she bids ten thousand.

It's over. Adrian goes for ten thousand euros. He throws out a kiss and wave to us all, turns, and strides back toward the stage curtains to make his exit.

"Woo-hoo!" Anna hollers. "Let's give another hand to Adrian!"

Everyone applauds wildly as he vanishes backstage. Servants swoop in to refresh our drinks. They memorized what we ordered earlier and bring us each more of the same. I haven't touched my glass of wine and turn down a second glass. It's the good stuff too. Very generous.

Anna lifts a hand for silence and then announces the

next prince. "Next up is Oscar, who some say should've been dubbed the royal hottie. Let me know if you agree."

Oscar rips the curtains open and spreads his arms wide. He's in a navy blue button-down shirt, dark gray dress pants, and leather shoes. Elegant, stylish, and sophisticated.

"Hello, ladies!" Oscar hollers. "Who's feeling lucky tonight?"

Maybe not so sophisticated. The sexy pickup line works though. The women go wild. They're out of their seats, hands in the air.

"Me-e-e!"

"I want to feel lucky!"

"You're hot!"

He's pointing at different women with an intense sexy expression, holding his hand to his heart like he felt the compliment deeply. Oh, he's good, interacting with the audience.

Oscar smiles, and the women let out a soft swoony sigh in near unison. His eyes sparkle as he takes them in. "I love you, ladies! You're fantastic, every last one of you, here for such a good cause!" He flashes a naughty grin and starts to unbutton his shirt.

Hooting and hollering erupts as he works his way down the buttons. Then with his shirt completely unbuttoned, he struts down the catwalk, the shirt playing peek-aboo with defined pecs and rippling abs.

The crowd goes berserk! My ears ring from the high-pitched screaming.

Anna barks over the noise, "Let's start the bidding! Can I hear one thousand?"

Oh, yeah. The bidding goes fast—one thousand, three, five, seven.

Oscar gets into it, lifting his arms and doing some hip gyrations that are sexy as fuck as he gazes into the eyes of whoever just bid the highest. The women are beside themselves. He knows how to work a crowd, that's for sure. I can't look away from the sexy display that's somehow over-the-top and engaging at the same time. He's inviting us in on the fun.

Bidding tops out at twelve thousand. Holy crap. Do these ladies know this is in euros? That's actually more than twelve thousand in US dollars. Maybe money isn't an issue for them. Anna did say they were all successful in their careers.

Another round of drinks circulates, the women chattering happily and laughing. I can't fully enjoy the fun, thinking of Phillip up there soon, having women drooling over him, someone else winning a date with him. Jealousy is an ugly thing. I want to be above it.

Next up is Lucas with his sexy beard. Not to be outdone by his younger brothers, Lucas appears on stage wearing a blazer over his dress shirt, which he promptly sheds, swings in a circle over his head, and tosses out to the crowd.

A woman leaps out of her seat to grab it. "Five thousand!" she hollers, blazer clutched in hand.

Wow. Anna hasn't even started the bidding yet.

Lucas gestures for the bidding to keep going, then makes a big show of unbuttoning his shirt, slowly undoing the top button. He stops, leans toward the crowd, and croons, "Should I keep going?"

"Yeah!"

"Take it all off!"

"Strip, strip, strip!"

Anna goes for it. "Do I hear six thousand?"

"Six thousand!" someone immediately puts in.

He slowly undoes the next button as more bids roll in. Then he struts down the catwalk, stopping a few times to give the grabbing hands of the women a squeeze. We're all on our feet. I'm only standing because otherwise I couldn't see a thing at my height. Okay, he's insanely hot. Is it the beard? The sexy confidence? Who cares?

"Only two princes left in need of a date," Anna says. "Who will be the lucky lady?"

Lucas returns to center stage, goes to the next button on his gaping shirt, and stops. "Want more?"

"Yes!" the women holler.

"Let's hear twelve thousand," he says with a grin.

"Twelve thousand! Yes!" a woman hollers.

He rips the shirt open, the buttons flying off. Sculpted tanned muscle from chest to abs. Whoa.

The bids instantly go up, up, up. Faster and faster, insane levels!

He closes the shirt and then flashes a pec. Someone screams like they're a teen at a rock concert. The women are crazy to have him, hollering out bids and his name.

He gestures for more bidding and, when he gets it, flashes his abs.

He closes his shirt and blows us a kiss. Then his hands go to his belt buckle. The crowd gasps before a flurry of excited bidding. He's trained them to bid and get a flash. He won't really do it, though, will he? I can't look away.

Someone screams, "Twenty thousand!" And that crazy woman rushes the stage to claim her prize.

The pack of women are hot on her heels, screaming more bids at Lucas as security closes in.

He just stands there, grinning.

7

Phillip

There's a brief intermission after my show-off brother caused a riot. Lucas was immediately hauled backstage while the sixteen sloshed horny women were escorted back to their seats. Ruby remained in her seat, staying above the fray. Thank God she's here. Gabriel stormed backstage too, as I predicted. He does not suffer fools, and Lucas took it too far. Anna has the women in the back of the room, where appetizers are waiting on a long table. She's talking to them in a loud voice, but I can't make out the words. I hope she's telling them I won't be stepping foot on stage if they can't behave themselves.

Lucas is unrepentant while Gabriel rips him a new one. It's not the same as being chastised by our father. Gabriel is still the big brother, who protected him from harsher truths his whole life. In any case, I know Lucas did it to win the bet and, if I don't top twenty thousand, he'll win the pool. My brothers didn't even bet a lot of money, just a couple of hundred euros. It's the principle of the thing. Sibling rivalry lives on in the Rourke family, at least among the men. My sisters are quite proper since my mother kept them on a tight leash. My father indulged us boys (besides Gabriel the heir) for the most part, seeing himself in us as the younger brother. But when my mother put her foot down on our antics, my father would step in, and his stern dictates felt extra sharp after so much casual indulgence. All of us would straighten up fast when my father got serious.

I doubt I'll top Lucas's bid. I won't be doing a striptease. Whatever the highest bid is, I'll give Anna the signal and have her top it by a small amount so Ruby can win me.

Gabriel storms offstage, muttering about "mob mentality."

The volume increases as the women get comfortable again, the music blasting from the DJ, probably to keep the energy high.

Adrian appears by my side. "Maybe show a little skin up there." He's still hoping to win the betting pool, and he bet on me.

"Princes don't strip for entertainment."

Adrian points at me. "You're already entertainment as the royal hottie. Give them something to make them crazy to buy you."

I'm beginning to hate that royal hottie title. I'm more than that. "I'm not for sale at any price."

One side of his mouth curls up. "Today you are. It's for a good cause, right? So give it your all. I have faith in you."

"You have a bet on me. There's a difference."

"Semantics."

"Wimp," Lucas says.

"Let him lose," Oscar says.

"Could you at least do some hip thrusts?" Adrian asks. "I know you could win if you tried."

My little brother urging me to do hip thrusts. Bizarre. "No."

Anna appears backstage. "Okay, guys, Gabriel is not happy." She takes in a deep breath. "To put it mildly. Lucas, I can't believe you were going to take off your pants."

Lucas is matter-of-fact. "I wanted to get them excited and bid high. And I didn't take them off. I merely hinted at it. It worked, didn't it?"

Anna gestures wildly. "I told you yesterday to keep it clean! If I wanted butt cheeks on display, I would've handed out G-strings!"

My brothers chuckle.

"There were no butt cheeks on display," Lucas says solemnly.

My brothers laugh out loud.

Anna is not happy. She scowls. "Gabriel threatened to shut the whole thing down and kick my guests out of the palace if I can't get them under control. Phillip still has to go on, and you know with his royal hottie rep he's the headliner. We need him to have his turn."

I turn to her. "Don't worry. Gabriel knows I'll keep it clean. He was just blowing off steam."

My brothers agree.

Anna smooths her hair. "I suppose you're right. I've just never seen him so angry. I had to talk him down before he yelled at our guests."

She's still relatively new to Gabriel, a newlywed, and doesn't fully grasp his warrior-like tendencies. "You know you married a relic, right?" I ask her.

Her brows shoot up. "A relic? He's only thirty."

"He's a throwback to our Viking ancestors. He should've been a warrior king. Ask him; he's always said that. You have to understand that's who he is on the inside, and everything else, the royal protocol and customs, are something he abides by only by sheer strength of will." I used to think duty was easy for him, until he recently spelled out exactly what it would be like if I took his place as king (in the case he abdicated to marry commoner Anna). My parents relented and allowed the marriage because Gabriel was groomed from the start to be king, none of us were as well prepared, and they understood love, having such a strong marriage themselves.

Anna looks thoughtful. "You know, that actually explains a lot. A warrior king." She goes up on tiptoe and kisses my cheek. "Thank you, Phillip. Knock 'em dead. Do whatever you want. I trust you."

I incline my head. "As you should. Could you direct security to stand closer to the catwalk?"

"Absolutely." She heads back through the curtains.

"You're seriously afraid of a small group of women?" Oscar asks.

"They're harmless," Adrian assures me. "They just want to get to know us. We're a novelty to them."

I cross my arms. "I'm not afraid. I just prefer not to be mauled. One of them already ripped the pocket right off my trousers for a souvenir. I wouldn't put it past them to rip my shirt or yank out a lock of my hair."

"And he's got such lovely locks too," Lucas teases, ruffling my hair.

I knock his hand away. "Piss off. If it weren't for you showing off, we wouldn't be dealing with a riot situation."

"Oh, please," Lucas says. "It's sixteen women."

"Seventeen. Ruby's here."

Lucas smirks. "Aha. I see where you're at." He turns to Oscar and Adrian. "Did you hear how he said her name?"

Adrian leans in. "Do you think she has the funds to win you?" He's still zeroed in on his stake in the betting pool.

I shrug one shoulder, not wanting to let on about my part in helping her win. "Maybe."

Adrian abruptly leaves. Now where is he going? He's not going to sweet-talk Ruby, is he? The whole point of me being here was to keep Adrian at a distance from her.

Anna's voice carries through the microphone. "Everyone back to their seats! We're about ready for the royal hottie—"

She's cut off by a high-pitched group scream and a mad scramble of high-heeled women to their seats. So much for calming everyone down; instead the brief intermission has built up the anticipation. The music lowers in volume, still a sexy thumping beat. I break out in a sweat and drag a hand through my hair. This feels too much like a performance, and I have never been a performer. One on one, hanging with friends at a party or a club, great. Going on stage, even in front of a small audience, no.

I eye the exit, the muscles in my legs tense, ready for escape.

No, it's for a good cause. For Anna. For Villroy. For my insane jealousy.

"Should we bring him out?" Anna hollers.

"Yes!" the women scream.

I suck in air, working on a calming deep breath.

Anna lowers her voice. "Let's let him know how much we want to see him. Royal hottie, royal hottie..."

The women pick up the chant. I will hear it in my nightmares forever. They get louder and louder and louder.

I wipe the sweat from my brow with my shirtsleeve.

Anna has to yell at the top of her lungs to be heard over the chanting. "Here he is, the one, the only, the man of the hour, the royal hottie!"

I can't move.

Someone gives me a shove. I turn and shove Lucas back. Oscar joins in, and they both push me forward. I shove them back with all my might, and we have a brief grappling match, two against one. I'm just furious enough to give them a fight. They release me suddenly, and the room goes quiet. *Uh-oh.*

I glance over my shoulder. The curtains have been fully pulled back—our brief wrestling match exposed.

"Come on out here, Phillip," Anna says. "We won't bite."

The women laugh.

I step forward on wooden legs, and the curtain closes behind me. I'm sure I'm emanating more anger than sexy approachability, but it can't be helped. I don't appreciate my little brothers trying to push me around. I don't care if they're not actually little anymore. I'm the older one and deserve their respect.

Anna signals for the music to lower. "Now, ladies, before we get to the bidding, I want to let you know what an honor it is for us to have Phillip here. He wasn't sure at first about my idea, but I won him over to the dark side."

The women whoop and whistle.

She smiles at me. I can't even force a smile while standing on stage in front of a pack of man-hungry riotous women. She turns back to the audience. "He's the total package, ladies. He loves women—"

"We love you, Phillip!"

"I love you!"

"Love me!"

Anna goes on. "And he's very involved in charitable work to bring clean water to poor communities. Not just by being their spokesperson, he's on the ground, going into villages, meeting tribal leaders, spending time with their people, helping to smooth the way. He's generous, doing good just for its own sake. So let's call him what he really is, a prince among men, a dream prince."

Crickets.

And then a voice calls out, "Yes!"

I zero in on Ruby sitting near the catwalk in the last row. She's leaning into the aisle so I can see her beautiful face. "Thank you, Ruby!"

She grins and gives me a thumbs-up.

Anna gestures for me to walk down the catwalk. "Do I hear fifty?" Wow, that is a really low bid after Lucas's crazy-high bids. Maybe she thinks the crowd has lost interest in the real me. I am a dream prince. And that is so much better than the objectifying title previously given to me.

Ruby raises her hand. "One hundred." She bid on me. My chest expands with pride. It's more than she bid on Adrian, even though she's broke. She wants me.

"How about two hundred?" Anna asks.

My eyes are only for Ruby as I walk down the catwalk in my buttoned shirt, leather trousers, and boots. Fully dressed dream prince here. It's definitely easier to do the walk focused on her familiar blond hair that just brushes the shoulders of her bright pink V-neck sweater. Her eyes are sparkling, her face lit up with a smile just for me. I'm dimly aware of women hollering numbers around me. Thousands.

Finally I reach her and drop to my haunches. "Thank you for the generous bid."

Her cheeks flush pink. "Uh, sure. I'm afraid I'm out of funds."

I lean down and whisper, "It's the thought that counts."

We smile at each other, and warmth spreads through me, calming my nerves.

I straighten and spread my arms wide to my adoring fans. "You rock, ladies! What a fantastic cause! How much can we help Anna with her good work?"

Anna immediately jumps in with, "Do I hear ten thousand?"

I turn and stride back down the catwalk, glad we're nearly done. I catch Anna's eye and cross my fingers at my side. She gets the message and holds up her cell phone. "I've got a bid here from an anonymous bidder. It's eleven thousand."

"Eleven thousand one hundred," a woman with sleek black hair counters.

I keep my fingers crossed, which means keep going.

"Eleven thousand two hundred from anonymous," Anna says.

"Twelve thousand," the woman says.

It keeps going from there, astonishingly high. I keep to my signal, even as the numbers get to teeth-clenching levels.

"Fifty thousand," Anna says.

Silence.

"Fifty thousand to the anonymous bidder!" Anna

exclaims. "Woo! Good work, ladies! And thank you so much, Phillip!"

I incline my head. I've just donated fifty thousand of my personal funds to the cause, but you know what? That's fine. It's an investment for Villroy. In fact, I'll donate even more than that. And I got what I wanted—Ruby.

"Okay, everyone, we're going to clear the chairs and boogie!" Anna hollers.

The music blasts, the spotlight on the stage turns off, and I go backstage. It's empty. My brothers have already left to mingle. I head into the room to do my part to mingle, and my guards flank me. I scan the room for Ruby, and then she's right there, heading toward me.

"You made it without causing a riot," she says, smiling up at me. "Great work."

I chuckle. "Thank you."

She gets serious. "So, uh, do you know who the bidder was who won a date with you?"

I give her a slow secret smile. "Anonymous."

"You don't know?"

I lean down to her ear. "I bid through Anna. You won me." I pull back to gauge her reaction. She looks stunned, her green eyes wide, her jaw slack. I tense. Shit. Maybe she doesn't want to go on a date with me.

I'm about to declare it would be completely platonic, no pressure, when she exclaims, "Phillip, you bid fifty thousand euros! This was supposed to be a fundraiser from outside sources."

I let out a quiet exhale, all of my muscles relaxing again. She was only worried about the money. "Villroy is my legacy. Of course I want to contribute."

She rubs the side of her neck and gives me a sideways

look. "You must've really wanted to go on a date with me. You could've just asked, you know."

I lower my voice. "I was also trying to avoid the man-hungry crowd. These women are nutso wild." And I needed to keep you away from Adrian, I silently add. I know he didn't egg her on with the bidding. She stopped at a hundred. What was he doing?

She laughs. "They're fun. I think Anna let them have too much to drink before feeding them. Woo!" She gestures with her arms spread wide. "Inhibitions out the window!"

"To put it mildly."

Someone claps me on the back. It's a grinning Adrian. I knew it had to be family; otherwise, the guards wouldn't let anyone touch me. I hadn't used security earlier when my trousers were ripped by grabbing man-hungry hands, and I probably should have.

"You beat them all!" he crows. He won the pool. Nothing thrills him more than winning.

I narrow my eyes at him. "Where did you go? Were you driving up the bidding somehow?"

He winks. "Who, me?"

"Adrian!"

"Relax, it's all for a good cause." He probably boosted the woman with the black hair's bid.

I shove his shoulder. "You should chip in personally, too."

"I will. We all plan to." He looks from me to Ruby and back to me. "Phillip, you sly dog, you were the anonymous bidder, weren't you?"

Heat creeps up my neck. It's one thing for Ruby to know, a whole other thing for my teasing brothers to know. "It was anonymous."

He grins. "Phillip, Phillip, Phillip, I had no idea you were such a romantic." He turns to Ruby. "What do you think? Is he worth fifty thousand euros for one lousy date?"

"Lousy!" I protest.

Ruby smiles mischievously. "Only one way to find out." Then she hugs me around the middle. I loop an arm over her shoulders and pull her close.

Adrian shakes his head. "Guess we do have a tradition of Rourkes falling for Americans. First our uncle abdicated for an American, and then Gabriel threatened to do the same. What is it about you Americans?"

Now the heat from my neck is all the way up to the tips of my ears, my heart pumping hard. I can't deny I'm into her, despite trying to keep my distance. Adrian just put it out there like a big red flag.

Ruby takes it in stride. "I guess us Americans are just plain awesome."

He chuckles. "You are." He heads to the bar and is quickly surrounded by women eager to get close to him.

I turn to Ruby. "I suppose I should join the party. Stick to my side."

"Ooh, I feel like one of your security guards, except I'm the *don't touch him, ladies, he's mine* kind of tough." She laughs. "I did win you."

I can't help but smile. Maybe it was okay that Adrian put it out there. Maybe we're on the same page. "That kind of toughness is exactly what I need." I take her hand, entwining our fingers together, and head to the bar.

The women immediately form a crowd around me. "Where are you going on your date?" the woman with black hair who bid on me asks.

"Paris," I say.

Ruby squeaks.

"Damn, I should've went higher," the black-haired woman says. "Adrian only gave me twenty-five grand."

Holy shit. That means she was willing to put up twenty-five grand of her personal funds. The total is more than double Lucas, and all I had to do was take a walk fully clothed. I am *the man*.

"He's mine now," Ruby says, wrapping an arm around my waist and leaning against my side. "I was the anonymous bidder."

"Why were you anonymous?" the woman asks. "You were in the room."

Ruby turns to me.

"She's shy." I can't think of anything better. I probably should've told Ruby not to share that she won me, though the mystery of an anonymous bidder would've been hard to avoid as a topic of conversation.

"Actually," Ruby says, "the truth is, I was a little embarrassed of the huge crush I have on him."

My head swivels toward hers, but she keeps her gaze fixed on the curious women.

She goes on. "We talked just a few minutes ago and he was so gracious I don't feel embarrassed anymore. I mean, I've followed him online for years—"

"Me too!" the woman says.

More women gather close to share in their mutual stalking of me.

"He's my screensaver," one woman says. "You know the picture of him on the beach at St. Bart's?"

I inwardly cringe. The women carry on as if I'm not standing there.

"Which one? Red trunks? Black?"

"Black. Wet and snug."

"Mmm-hmm, fi-i-i-ne."

"Oh, that's a good one!"

"You can make out the outline…"

They snicker and stare at my crotch. I pull Ruby in front of me and wrap my arms around her waist. She rests a hand on my forearm and gives me a small squeeze.

"What did you ladies think of Lucas?" Ruby asks, turning the conversation. "Think he would've taken off more if we'd kept our distance?" She's clever, including herself in the riot to get them talking. She sat in the back the whole time.

The women immediately chime in their opinions on his stripping possibility and what that might reveal. It's much raunchier than the talk about me.

I lean down and kiss Ruby's cheek, feeling her smile as her cheek curves. She feels right in my arms, and I'm more comfortable than I thought I'd be in this bizarre situation. I should've seen the signs—the chemistry, my need to be near her, my uncharacteristic jealousy. I'm falling for her, even though it's a dead end. I can't seem to stop it, the slow roll into a crash. She's irresistible.

8

Ruby

I'm hyper, flushed and excited, totally thrown by the turn of events. First, that Phillip wanted me enough to bid sky-high to go on a date with me. And, second, by the fact that Adrian shared that Phillip is falling for me and Phillip seemed to agree. All of these feelings are pouring out of me—affection, warmth, deep like, no, it's worse than that. We've been at the bar for an hour now, mingling with the ladies and his brothers, and every time he turns and smiles at me, my stomach actually gets butterflies. There's fluttering up there and more fun going on down below. I want him so bad.

Anna grabs my hand and tugs me along with her. "This is my song! Dance floor, ladies! You too, guys!"

I laugh and join her. It's Justin Timberlake's "Can't Stop the Feeling!" Just her kind of upbeat fun song. Everyone joins us, except for the guards and Gabriel. Phillip moves in by my side. He's a good dancer. I've seen pictures of him dancing at clubs. I square off with him, and he dances close, his hands moving in the air around my body. It's electric, the heat simmering between us.

I lift my hands over my head and let go, moving my body sensuously, feeling sexy for the first time since the horrible breakup breakdown. I'm back from the dead and ready to throw myself at life, at him.

Slow down. It's a dance, it's one date, it's one week.

He slips an arm around my waist, drawing me close, his leg wedging between mine as we grind. Oh, fuck, yes. His aquamarine eyes are intent on mine, heated and sure.

"Hello?" Anna says, appearing next to us. "You two want to take this upstairs?"

Phillip immediately pulls away. I glare at Anna.

She sends me a significant look. It's a reminder. *Don't think you can fix the manwhore. He'll only hurt you.* I look away, in denial, because right now I feel awesome with Phillip.

Anna gestures in a big *get over here* move to Gabriel, who's watching her from the side of the dance floor. "Your Majesty, get your cute butt over here!"

Phillip and I exchange an amused look. Anna informed me earlier she's not supposed to swear in public now that she's queen. Normally she'd say ass.

I glance over at Gabriel. A smile plays over his lips, his gaze warm on Anna, but he doesn't budge.

She dances over to him and, a moment later, he's dancing a waltz with her, completely wrong for this song, but Anna doesn't seem to mind.

I go back to dancing with Phillip. Other women have crowded around him now that there's space. His gaze returns to me again and again, and I can't find it in me to be jealous. He wants me as much as I want him.

The song changes to a slow one. Phillip and I immediately lock gazes. He crosses to me, takes my hand, and pulls me close, his other arm banding around my waist. He doesn't ask if I want to dance with him. He doesn't need to.

I glance around the dance floor. His brothers are all paired off. Some of the women do twirling dances with each other, laughing. Some of them head back to the bar.

He's moving us, subtly, slowly shifting us to the edge of the crowd. All of my nerve endings light up in anticipation. He probably wants to bail, go somewhere private with me, but then he stops a small distance from the group and continues our dance.

"Are we going upstairs after this?" I blurt.

"No."

"Oh." I'm confused. He arranged for our date and he's been affectionate with me tonight.

His voice is a husky rumble in my ear. "Ruby, I like you a lot, but I'm leaving in a week, so are you. I won't be returning for a very long time. And the truth is, I don't do relationships. I find you tempting, so damn tempting, but I want to do right by you. I want to be better than my reputation."

My throat gets tight, and I swallow hard. Even turning me down, he does it for noble reasons. I know I shouldn't give him a pass on his well-deserved reputation, but it's really hard not to when he's being so honest and forthright. He's not taking advantage, he's protecting my feelings. "Maybe I wasn't looking for a relationship."

He draws me close. "You'd regret it. I know that much about you."

I can't let it go. "Maybe I just wanted a little fun for the short time I have here. Once I get home, I'll be busy with my new business. I really want to hit the ground running so I can afford my own place. I've been living with my parents since I lost my job. Soon I'll have a baby sister, and my parents need my room."

He pulls back to meet my eyes. "A baby sister? That's quite an age gap."

"I know. She's a miracle. We're all so excited, and I don't want to miss out on a thing. She's the sister I've always wanted." I take a deep breath. "So maybe just for tonight—"

"Our paths likely won't cross again, and I don't want to hurt you."

My voice comes out small. "So just one date?"

He looks over my shoulder. "We can spend time together during your stay. As friends."

I can't keep the frustration from my voice. "You've been more than friendly tonight."

"I can't seem to help myself, but I know the right thing to do." He puts some space between us, finally meeting my eyes. "I want to be a good memory for you."

I let out an exaggerated sigh. "You really are a prince."

He laughs and pulls me into a hug. "I suppose so." He pulls back and holds me by the shoulders. "Still want to go on that date with me?"

I force a smile, my eyes hot. "Paris? Duh. Of course I want to go to Paris."

He resumes the dance. "Good."

"So do I get a goodnight kiss on this date?"

He hesitates. "Sure."

"Second base?"

He pulls back enough to look at me. "Oh, Ruby, you're on a slippery slope, I'm afraid."

"Don't be scared. I'll be gentle."

He smirks. "That's my line."

We dance in silence, our bodies close, heated, drawn together despite the line he's drawn. I don't think I can resist the temptation that is Phillip. He's turned into my dream prince, and I don't want to miss out. The fact that I leave in a week makes it urgent that I have him while I still can.

I go up on tiptoe to whisper in his ear, "What if I told you, no matter what, there would only be good memories. That I would treasure our time together and know it for what it was, a temporary thing."

He stills, and hope soars within me. And then he drops his arms from me and steps back. "It wouldn't be that simple."

"Why not? We could agree ahead of time."

We stare at each other, the short distance between us feeling like a giant chasm that can never be crossed.

Lucas appears at my side. "Hey, big spender, I heard it was you who won Phillip. How about a dance? Or are you two still dancing?" He looks at Phillip standing a distance away.

"Go ahead," Phillip says and heads to the bar.

I go cold.

Lucas takes my hand and leads me in a waltz. He's a good dancer and leaves a polite distance. Yet I can't enjoy myself, can't take my eyes off Phillip at the bar. The women have gathered around him and he's chatting with them. How can he deny us? What if what we have —our intense attraction, our warm friendship—is not so easy to find again? What if it's unique and this is a chance of a lifetime? Am I really just going to let him go? Would that be the smart thing to do, or a foolish mistake?

"He likes you," Lucas says as if he could read my

mind. Or maybe I'm just that obvious with my longing looks at his brother.

"I like him too."

"His ex wrecked him," he says. "Serious baggage." Is that why Phillip said it wouldn't be that simple? Because he has real feelings for me, and he's the one who doesn't want to get hurt?

"I get that. I've been through similar."

He whistles out a long breath. "That could be bad. Two people with serious baggage. Sounds like a minefield."

"What if it's worth the risk?"

"Sometimes it is. Sometimes it's brutal."

"You know this from personal experience?"

He steps away and does a courtly bow. "Thank you for the dance." He goes to ask another woman to dance, who's been standing on the sidelines.

I let out a breath. Now I'm not sure what to do. Go to Phillip? Ignore him? But then he's striding toward me, his guards flanking him, and I know there's no real decision to be made. I must be with him.

Phillip

I tried to resist for Ruby's benefit, okay, for mine too, but I was fighting the inevitable. Whatever this is, I can't keep away for the short time I've been granted with her. The moment Lucas abandoned her on the dance floor, I went to her. Now I'm leading her through the east wing and up to the flat rooftop garden accessible only to the royal family. It's my favorite spot in the palace.

"Oh, wow, look at the view!" she exclaims, rushing

toward the far end, where the crashing waves along the beach are visible in the distance.

"You can see the whole island from up here on a clear night." I look up just as a cloud passes over the moon, dimming the light. "It's a little cloudy but still good."

She goes to the edges of the space, looking all around, before turning to me. "So what do you do up here?"

"Usually we party."

A couple of servants appear through the door, William and John. I requested they bring a few items. William is holding a chilled bottle of the same sauvignon blanc Ruby had earlier and two glasses. John has a couple of plush throw blankets to ward off the chill of a late September night.

I maneuver one of the chaise lounges in front of the ocean view and accept the blankets. John brings a matching chaise lounge next to mine and then a small wooden table, where William sets the wine and glasses.

I gesture for Ruby to take a seat. She looks delighted as she sinks into the cushioned seat. I settle one of the blankets over her lap.

"Thank you!" she exclaims. "This is perfect!"

I take the seat next to her and stretch the blanket out over my legs. William opens the wine and pours a glass for both of us.

"Will there be anything else, Your Highness?" he asks.

"This is good, thank you."

They both bow and take their leave.

Ruby takes a sip of her wine. "Ahh. This is the life."

"I love it up here. So peaceful. Do you want me to put the floor lights on?"

"No. The stars and moon are just right. So tell me what we're going to do on our date."

"I thought we'd take the jet to Paris…" I trail off, alarmed at her coughing fit. "Are you okay?"

She leans close, her eyes watering. "It went down the wrong pipe when I gasped. We're taking a private jet to Paris?"

"Did you think us poor?"

"I didn't think much about it. A private jet?"

"Yes. Anna's fundraiser wasn't because we didn't have the funds. It was cleverly designed to involve the people who will later become future clients of the spa. She's hoping they'll spread the word about it."

She smiles. "She's a smart cookie, isn't she?"

"Yes. A natural entrepreneur, and my brother is behind her, using his own considerable power and connections to smooth the way."

She takes a sip of wine and sighs. "I love that she's queen and has all of you. She had a rough childhood and, well, I know she's always wanted family."

"She'll probably have her own family with Gabriel soon. They're getting started on the heir right away."

"Oh, that's wonderful! She'll be the best mom."

"Agreed."

"Okay, so after we jet off to Paris, then we…"

"Dine at L'Ambroisie and then—"

"Wait, tell me about the restaurant."

"The chef is a family friend, he's been around forever, and it's a three-star Michelin restaurant. For foodies, that's the ultimate. You pass through the seventeenth-century arcades of Places des Vosges to enter the restaurant. You'll love that." At her puzzled look, I backtrack to what might've been unfamiliar to her. "Places des Vosges is like a park, a residential square of open space surrounded by redbrick apartment buildings with shops and restaurants below. The street level of the buildings has these large arches, they're called arcades. Anyway, you loved the historic shopping mall at Nantes so much, I thought you'd really like it. And then once you're inside, the interior is an elegant Viennese style."

"Describe it."

I try to picture it in my mind's eye. "White wood paneling, gold-trimmed mirrors, silk tapestries, crystal chandeliers, round tables with white tablecloths, red and purple velvet chairs, marble patterned floors. I'm sure I'm not doing it justice. You'll have to see it in person."

"It sounds like you picked this date special for me. What if someone else had won you?"

"Then I would've had a candlelit dinner in the royal dining room and invited everyone—my brothers, sister, and the other guests—up here for a party. Very little alone time."

She gives me a small pleased smile and sips her wine.

I sip mine too. I don't mind that I've shown my hand, and she knows I'm into her. I want her to know. I want to treat her special. "So after that, we could go dancing at a club, or we could come back here and relax on the rooftop garden. Or walk on the beach. Really up to you. I want you to experience everything you're interested in here as a newcomer."

She smiles. "That's a nice way to say I'm a tourist. I'd like dinner, dancing, and then back here to the rooftop garden." She looks off in the distance and sighs. "You're not like the guys I usually meet."

"I suppose I'm your first royal."

She laughs. "Yes, but I mean, you just seem more direct, more expressive than most guys."

I look off in the distance before confiding, "I wasn't

always the playboy prince. I did commit once. It ended in a very public breakup. So maybe I was happy with my scandalous reputation. My ex could see I was doing just fine without her." I turn to her. "Lately, though, I'm really starting to hate it. I wanted my charitable work to help clean up my image for the sake of my family, but now I want to change it just as much for me."

She gives me a sympathetic look. "I heard about Lana."

I take a swallow of wine to ease the tightness in my throat. "Yes, well, everyone did."

My breakup with Lana was extremely public, covered by all the gossip rags, all over the internet, so I'm sure Ruby knows the basics. Lana and I were the golden couple for five years and then she dumped me *by text* for a Greek billionaire, whom she said she loved. They were plastered all over the gossip rags too. Now, a little over a year later, I hear she's single and I get a sick satisfaction out of knowing that. I hope he dumped her as callously as she dumped me. I guess I haven't completely gotten over it if I'm still bitter. I'm not that evolved.

We're quiet for a few minutes, but it's not awkward. Lana fades from my mind as I find peace again, sitting next to Ruby, cozy and warm, gazing at the sea.

"I feel like a different person sitting up here on this peaceful island," she says, breaking the silence. "Like I'm not just buffeted by forces beyond my control. Like I'm in control. Maybe it's because I've been working on my first big solo project here. I like working for myself."

"You're great at your job."

"Thanks. Anna did me a huge favor calling me for it. Plus she bragged about me to all her friends when she gave them the tour. They all want me to do projects for them when I get back to Tampa. It'll really get my business off the ground."

"That's fantastic!"

"It is. Things are finally looking up."

I look over at her and she turns, our gazes locking for a charged moment.

She looks away and takes a big swallow of wine. "What was it like growing up here?"

I take a sip of wine and then set it down. No one wants to hear a prince complain about duty, obligation, and public scrutiny. I was born into wealth and never wanted for anything. "It was great. I know I'm blessed."

She leans in. "That sounds like a canned answer for the press. Tell me what it was really like."

"I appreciate everything I have. My brothers and I had fun running around the island, exploring the dunes and caves, swimming and surfing in the waves."

"Don't forget cruising around on the yacht."

I grin. "That was more of a launching pad to dive into the sea. Of course, we took out the jet skis too."

"Of course!"

"See, it sounds like luxury. It was. Like I said—"

"I know, I know, you appreciate what you have. What's it like to have no privacy? To have your every move documented and commented on?"

"I learned to embrace it. I'm a people person and, while it's intrusive at times, for the most part I don't mind."

"Even with your ex?"

"I loved being part of the golden couple. It seemed everyone loved us together as much as I did. I thought we'd marry, and then we didn't." My voice chokes. "I seem to pick beautiful, vain, shallow women. Maybe so I won't be tempted to commit." I pause, surprising myself with the insight. I never proposed to Lana, and I set up everything for maximum sabotage with other women for more than a year now. I press my lips together before admitting the truth. "Maybe I'm just not cut out for commitment."

She gives my hand a squeeze. "Anyone would take a breather from commitment after her. I know she dumped you for a really old guy, so guess what? You're better off. She sounds like a gold digger, and maybe she knew your kingdom wasn't doing so well economically."

"She did know that. And I'm glad they broke up."

"Ha-ha. Sweet revenge. I wish bad things for my ex too, even though I feel guilty because he's about to be a father to triplets with his wife."

I straighten. "His wife?"

"Yup. I was the other woman, though I didn't know it. We lived together for a year. A *whole year*, Phillip, where I was stupidly, ignorantly happy."

"I'm sorry."

"Yeah, me too." She sits up and says fiercely, "When he told me he was leaving me because his wife was expecting triplets, he wanted me to be happy for him! I'm just standing there, stunned, and then he says, 'By the way, you have to move out. This is my parents' vacation condo and they're coming for a visit because of the triplets. We're all so excited!'" She downs her wine in one long swallow. "Well, *I* was not excited. I was devastated."

My heart aches for her. I feel her pain. I know that kind of pain. "Shit. That sounds awful."

She sighs and relaxes into her chair again. "Yeah, it was. I lost my job because I just couldn't function. I moved back in with my parents, trying to get a freelance career going—mostly recovering—and now here I am two months later in a completely different headspace. At last, the cloud has lifted. I have a real chance at a cool career on my terms. I'll be able to get my own place, and they'll have my room for the baby. Everything is working out just as I hoped."

I take a deep breath. "It seems we met at the wrong time."

She studies me for a long moment, and I get a bad feeling that she's about to stomp on my heart. "I really like you."

"I like you too."

"But I think you had the right idea before. Neither of us is up for more devastation. We're still recovering. At least I am. And I know I said let's go for it for a one-week happy memory, but that was lust talking." Her gaze searches mine. "We can be smarter than that. I mean, you're still recovering from Lana, right?"

"Yes." I must be if I'm so spitefully glad Lana was dumped.

"And we're going our separate ways soon."

I exhale sharply. Why couldn't I have met Ruby a year ago? Except I'm just kidding myself. I couldn't have committed a year ago any more than I could now. I'd sabotage it in some way and end up hurting her. Maybe I'm only drawn to her because I know we have no future.

Silence falls. We both gaze out at the sea. There's nothing more to be said. There is no us and there never will be.

I turn to her. "Tell me what it was like growing up in Tampa."

She smiles and takes my hand, clasping it warmly on top of the blanket as she tells me of her orange trees, the warm waters of the Gulf, and her visits to the happiest place on earth, which inspired her love of interior design.

We end up talking all night, sitting side by side in the moonlight, holding hands.

We watch the sunrise together, and it's the best night of my life.

She stands and stretches as the sun finishes its rise in the sky. "I can't believe we talked until sunrise! You should've told me to shut up."

I stand and fold the blankets. "Never. I loved hearing all your stories."

"Thank you. I loved hearing yours too. And now I need sleep."

I walk her to the door, holding it open for her, and then walk her to her room. She stops just outside her door and tips her face up, smiling at me. "Thanks for a wonderful night."

I can barely breathe, so enthralled with her. "Thank *you*." I lean down to kiss her cheek, and she shifts, her lips meeting mine in a soft kiss.

I pull back in surprise. We agreed to be just friends.

She grabs my head and kisses me again. The blood rushes through my veins. I pin her against the door in a flash, the building tension finally having an outlet. Her lips are soft, her taste like wine and sex; it's a potent combination. She's gripping my hair, her nails digging into my shoulder, her tongue tangling with mine.

"Walk of shame, huh?" a feminine voice calls in a teasing voice.

I break the kiss and glare at one of Anna's friends in a jacket, yoga leggings, and sneakers, probably going out for an early run.

"I wish," Ruby says with a laugh.

My heart thunders in my chest, adrenaline pumping, all of me ready to move forward with this. Forget what we said before. I want her *now*.

The woman laughs and continues on her way.

Ruby holds up a palm to me, holding me off. "Good night and good morning." She slips inside and shuts the door behind her.

I consider following her in. I don't think she'd resist if I kissed her again. It would naturally lead to her bed. And then what? We screw our brains out for one week, getting in deeper and deeper, and then cut each other loose?

I turn away, heading to my suite. Neither of us is up for the devastation. She was right about that. I rub my aching chest. Maybe it's already too late. My body is denied, but my heart is out there, still with Ruby.

9

Ruby

Phillip has been a dream. After our all-night rooftop talk, we spent the rest of the week together, exploring the island and talking, talking, talking. It wasn't exactly private. He has two guards with him whenever he goes out, on the king's orders, not because he wants them. He swears the islanders would never hurt him. I got used to his guards, Henry and Rafe, once Phillip assured me they would never repeat anything they heard us say unless our lives were in danger. After a while, I forgot they were there and spoke freely. Being with Phillip is almost like hanging with a close friend, except for the sexual tension. It's always there, a subtle current running between us.

Now we're on the jet on the way to Paris for the date I won in the bachelor auction. Phillip is chatting with the flight attendant, asking after her family. I look out the window at the island fading in the distance. It's beautiful, a jewel of purple heather meadows, dunes, grassy slopes, and rugged cliffs in a sapphire sea setting. Amalie Palace looks enchanting—sandstone with copper roofs, multiple towers, and spires—perched on a hill in the center of the island. Cute cottages dot the long winding palace road. Soon this will all be like something I dreamed. I leave in two days. Phillip leaves the day after.

He turns to me, his blue-green eyes warm on mine. "It's a short flight. Just under an hour. There's a driver waiting for us. We'll do dinner and dancing and then head back. Does that all sound good?"

I search his features, hardly believing how familiar he feels to me after just two weeks. His thick dark brown hair with a natural wave to it, his sharp cheekbones and jawline, straight nose, his sensual full lower lip. God, he's a good kisser. We haven't kissed since our all-night talk and I miss it terribly. I tried and he gently explained I'm too tempting to open that door again. I don't care what anyone says, he is not some jerk manwhore only looking out for number one. Not with me. His rep is more a consequence of his bad breakup than who he really is. He even said he was starting to hate that rep. Deep down, he's a romantic at heart. Just look at how he planned this date around what I would like. He's so warm and attentive with me. That can't possibly be an act put on for seduction. He hasn't pushed for anything physical. In fact, just the opposite. And I know our lives are heading in different directions, but I simply can't deny myself any longer.

He leans close. "What's wrong?"

I worry my lower lip. "What if we skipped the dancing?"

"Oh. Okay. I'll have to call the club. I booked a private area for us." He pulls out his phone. "Is there something else you want to do?"

I nod.

He punches a few buttons on his phone. "What?"

"You."

His head jerks up. "You want to do…" Understanding dawns. He smirks and then shakes his head. "Ruby, I thought we—"

"I don't care," I whisper. "I'm leaving in two days. I can't leave never knowing what it's like to be with you."

He gives me a cocky smile. "It's fantastic."

I laugh. "I don't doubt that for a moment."

He gazes into my eyes. "Be sure. I don't want you to have regrets."

"No regrets. Paris is our little bubble. We can do whatever we want there, and when we leave, it's only with good memories."

"We'll always have Paris."

"Extra points for the *Casablanca* reference."

He smooths a lock of hair behind my ear. "If I knew we were going to have a Paris bubble, I would've brought you here days ago instead of playing tour guide on Villroy."

"One night. That's what makes it a bubble. A onetime thing."

"One night, not one time." He holds me by the chin and kisses me gently and then nips my lower lip. "Done." Then he gets on the phone, punches a few buttons, and speaks in rapid French, arranging what is no doubt going to be a primo hotel. All I care about is finally letting go with him. No more holding back.

~

The restaurant is everything Phillip described from the

moment I step through the arcade at Place des Voges to entering the restaurant with its elegant decor. It's like I stepped back in time to mingle in the parlor with high society. I'm so glad I brought my little black dress. This place is high class. No detail is overlooked, and I try to take it all in without gawking—gold-framed silk tapestries, gilded mirrors, crystal drop chandeliers, marble flooring with artfully placed Persian rugs. Each table is set elegantly with a white tablecloth, crystal wineglasses, china dishes, an abundance of silverware, and a small crystal vase of fresh flowers. I take Phillip's lead for what silverware goes with which dish. He was born to this; I'm just along for the ride.

What Phillip left out of his restaurant description is that the food is a frigging work of art! I didn't know food could look so stylish. It's almost too gorgeous to eat! My appetizer is scallops arranged in a circle in a spring pea soup with some fresh herbs and a purple flower in the center. I take a picture of it before I ruin the arrangement, which makes Phillip laugh.

I love absolutely everything, and Phillip is kind enough to share samples of his dishes. He ordered rack of lamb and I ordered the sole. And how cute is this? My potato pancake had little baby asparagus heads popping out of it! My absolute favorite is dessert. Mine looks like a cream puff cut in half, but in the center is a two-layer chocolate cake with a thick layer of sweet mango cream. Phillip's dark chocolate tart is also to die for. I probably could've finished off both desserts myself because, while the dishes were the highest quality, they were not big portions. This is food to savor.

The chef, a man in his seventies, even came out of the kitchen to see how we were enjoying our dinner. He and

Phillip chatted for a bit in French. I wish I knew something to say beyond *bonjour* and *merci beaucoup*.

After dinner, we take a walk through the city with his guards. I've never been here before, and it's a lot to take in, but my mind keeps skipping ahead to later—the hotel, the bed, a naked Phillip. I'm not nervous like I normally would be going to bed with a guy for the first time. I just feel excited. We've gotten to know each other well over the last two weeks. He's a good man and my gut says to trust him.

He's playing tour guide now, and I try to remember to say "cool" and "oh, really" at regular intervals.

He stops suddenly and turns me toward him, his hands gripping my upper arms. "Ruby, where are you? Am I boring you with the tour?"

I glance at his guards standing behind him. They discreetly look away.

I go on tiptoe and whisper, "I keep thinking about the hotel. Will Henry and Rafe be joining us there?"

He grins. "Yes, but they'll be posted outside the room, near the access points."

I keep my voice low. "Will they be able to hear us?"

His eyes dance with amusement. "Depends on how noisy you are."

"Me? What about you?"

"They're used to me."

I park a hand on my hip. "So this is like a regular thing for you?"

He cocks his head. "Now see, this is a trick question. If I say yes, you'll be pissed. If I say no, I'm lying to you. I don't want to lie to you, Ruby."

I press my lips together, irritated, but then a laugh escapes. "I know your rep."

He tips my chin up and kisses the end of my nose. "And you know I want to tone it down."

"Okay. Just take me to the hotel."

He turns to the guards. Henry nods once. "The car is already on its way."

I shake my head at Henry and Rafe. "How much you must know. You're very good at being discreet."

"Thank you, ma'am," Henry says, still stone-faced.

"It's our job, ma'am," Rafe says flatly.

"Okay, then." I turn to Phillip and whisper, "If I get loud, feel free to do one of these." I put my hand over my mouth.

He laughs and scoops me up in a hug, lifting me right off the ground. "It's our bubble, Ruby, do whatever you want."

A short while later, we arrive at the Ritz. Naturally. See, this Paris bubble will be a snap. It already feels like I'm moving through a dream. So different from my life back home I can't even wrap my brain around it.

Phillip takes my hand and leads me to the front desk. The clerk recognizes him immediately and quickly checks him in, handing over the key.

"They already knew what you wanted?" I whisper.

"I let them know ahead of time. I booked the Suite Imperiale. I thought you'd enjoy the historic interior since you're an interior designer and you loved Amalie Palace so much."

I'm practically vibrating with excitement. This is the kind of thing I don't see back home. European historic decor is much older and much more elegant than our oldest stuff, basically colonial America. We're still a pretty young country relatively speaking.

"Will you be needing any assistance with your

luggage, Your Highness?" the clerk inquires in perfect English.

Phillip responds cordially, "It's just us, thank you." He has zero embarrassment about using the hotel for sex, so why should I?

I follow him to our suite, the guards close behind. He holds the door open for me; I step inside and gasp. It's more like an apartment! This place is huge!

He shuts the door behind us. The guards remain in the hall.

His arms wrap around my waist from behind. "Well?"

"It's fantastic!"

"Go see the master bedroom. It's a replica of Marie-Antoinette's room at Versailles. It's the one done mostly in gold."

I rush through the living room with its two seating areas and head straight for a bedroom. This must be it. Everything in here is silk and gilded. It's eighteenth-century sumptuous elegance. The place is practically a museum with antique furniture and framed oil paintings. The bed is incredible with a carved headboard and foot-board, covered in silks, and set behind it is a gilded balustrade, like an elaborate canopy reaching up to the high ceiling. I pull out my phone, snapping pictures. I'm such a tourist.

I do a slow circle in the room. There's also a chaise longue, high-back antique chairs, multiple antique tables, a huge fireplace with an oil painting of a dark-haired man featured over it, probably Marie-Antoinette's husband, the king. I don't know my French history. I look up. Crystal chandelier, intricate plaster designs on the ceiling and molding, everything trimmed in gold. It's beyond, just *beyond*. I'm dying here. If I had seen this before I added my touch to the royal fantasy suite, I might've thrown my hands up, knowing how far I was from the mark of royal elegance.

I turn to Phillip, who followed me in. "Amazing! Is it weird I'm taking pictures instead of getting naked?"

He laughs. "Take as many pictures as you want. You're practically drooling. I knew this room would be a good choice. Look around your fill. I'm not going anywhere."

I do a slow tour of the suite, starting back in the living room. Two deep red sofas with gold tassels along the lower edges form two seating areas, back to back, separated by a long antique carved wood table. Glass doors lead to a balcony with a view of the city. I keep going toward a set of white double doors (French doors we call them back home) that lead to another bedroom, not as elaborate as the master, but still gorgeous, done in pale blues and pinks. Silk and gold trim abound in here too. An en suite bathroom mostly done in marble is beautiful, which makes me think the master bedroom's bathroom will be even better. I backtrack, heading through the master bedroom.

Phillip is hanging his suit jacket in a closet and winks at me as I go past him. He's such a sweetheart, patiently waiting for me.

Finally, I step into the bathroom. "Yes-s-s," I say on a long dreamy sigh. I gaze my fill at a huge marble-trimmed whirlpool tub big enough for two below a high window. There's a fireplace in here too, along with a table covered in luxury bath oils and lotions. White roses in a gold bowl on a vanity table lend a soft floral scent. Carved light wood paneling on every wall. There's another door. I peek into it to find the rest of the bathroom, all marble and elegant as expected. I return to the glorious soaking-tub area. It's like a spa in a museum. Unbelievable!

I can only imagine how much it costs to stay here. It must be thousands a night. I know I could never stay here on my own. Phillip really does live in a different world. And Paris is our bubble. I already feel like I'm floating outside myself, looking down at this extraordinary luxury that has never crossed even the far reaches of my imagination.

"What do you want to do first?" he asks from behind me, and I jump. He laughs. "Don't tell me you're nervous. This was all your idea." I can hear the smile in his voice, the teasing warmth.

I turn and laugh a little. "You startled me. My mind was blown in the master bedroom and I've been walking around in a trance ever since."

"I'm glad you like it. You want to take a bath?"

"By myself?"

"If you like. Or we could do a soak after…"

I close the distance and wrap my arms around his neck. "You're awfully accommodating. You should've had me under you the moment the door shut behind us."

He slides a warm hand under my hair and cups the back of my neck. "I don't want to rush. I want to savor you."

I sigh. Is it any wonder I'm falling for him?

He dips his head, his lips sealing over mine, his arm banding around my waist, drawing me tight against him. The kiss slides from tender to hungry in a flash, the familiar urgency rushing through me as I strain to get closer, only this time I don't have to stop. He doesn't have to stop. He's backing me up as he kisses me, until we get to the wall, and then he shoves my dress up to my waist and lifts me. *Yes.* This is so much better, everything lining up perfectly now. I wrap my arms and legs around him. He's got one hand on my jaw, holding me in place for his devouring mouth, his other hand sliding down my throat, across my collarbone, cupping my breast and flicking across my hard nipple. I moan in the back of my throat.

He shifts, kissing his way across my jaw down the side of my neck. I want more, more of him, more skin. I unbutton his white dress shirt to find a white crew-neck undershirt. "Too many clothes," I protest. "Get this stuff off."

He kisses me, nipping my lower lip, before smiling against my mouth. "No rush, remember?"

I yank his shirt from the waistband of his pants. "You're pissing me off."

He smirks and sets me back on my feet. Then I watch as he peels off the dress shirt and undershirt and tosses them on the vanity table. My mouth goes dry at the male beauty, so much beauty. "I love your shoulders," I blurt. "So wide and bulky with muscle."

His lips curve up. "Thank you."

A chime sounds and then a sharp rap at the door. My hand flies to my throat, my heart racing. "Is it the guards? Is something wrong?"

"Relax. I'm sure it's just the champagne I ordered."

He heads out toward the living room and opens the door, completely fine answering it shirtless. He's whistling a moment later. I join him in the living room just as he turns and opens a cabinet, pressing a few buttons. Soft jazz plays through speakers I hadn't noticed before.

He looks at me over his shoulder, a smile playing over his lips. "You seem a little jumpy, so I'm setting the scene for seduction."

"Oh, really?"

"Mmm-hmm." He adjusts the volume on the music, raising it high. He says something to me, but I can't make out the words over the music.

I cup a hand near my ear, heading toward him. "What?"

"Exactly!" He gestures to a marble table with the champagne and a gold box tied with brown and red ribbon.

"You got me a present?"

He wraps his arms around me from behind and whispers in my ear, "Chocolate truffles from the best chocolatier in Paris."

I melt. He remembered I love chocolate truffles. We have spent a lot of time talking, getting to know each other. I put a hand to my stomach. "If only I wasn't so stuffed from dinner."

"It'll be a good pick-me-up later when you're worn out from my thorough fucking."

My stomach drops, a low ache in my womb. It's the first time he's spoken crudely, and I like that it makes him feel more real and less perfect dream prince.

He brushes my hair to the side and kisses his way along my neck. I soften, all of my muscles warm and languid, desire unfurling within me. He gives my earlobe a tug with his teeth before whispering, "Music takes care of any noises you feel moved to make, the champagne is chilling, and the guards will remain posted on this end of the suite far from the master bedroom."

I turn in his arms. "Won't they hear the loud music and know it's to cover our sex noises?"

"I told them we're reciting French poetry," he says

with a straight face. "They were so disgusted they put in earplugs."

I crack up, and he smiles. "Are they really wearing earplugs?" I know it's a stretch, but I'd relax so much more if they were.

He doesn't answer. Instead he takes my hand and leads me to the bedroom. He stops next to the bed and shifts behind me, slowly unzipping the back of my dress, his fingers trailing lightly along my spine, giving me a shiver. I stare at the elegant bed done up in gold silk and blurt, "It's too nice a bed to mess up."

"Would you prefer the floor?"

"It's a Persian rug!" I strip all the covers off, so it's just the silk sheets, and look around for a safe place to set them.

Phillip takes them from my hands and sets them over a chair, giving me a wry look. "I'm beginning to think we should've booked the Holiday Inn."

I laugh. "Sorry."

"Don't be sorry, be naked." He slides my dress down and off and helps me step out of it. I reach for his belt buckle, but he shifts away.

His voice is rough. "Let me look at you." I try not to fidget, knowing I'm petite, not overly curved anywhere, really. Smaller than some guys prefer.

His eyes eat me up, starting at my black lace bra down to my matching panties and black heels. "So beautiful, Ruby. So damn sexy."

And I feel beautiful with him. I throw myself in his arms and then we're kissing passionately, his hands all over me. I break the kiss and refocus on getting him naked, undoing his belt. This time he lets me. Then I've got the clasp and zipper and finally I stroke him. He moans and tips his head back. I go for it, stripping him down to his socks. He's magnificent, his thick erection jutting out toward me, his legs powerful and muscular. He peels off the socks, and I step out of my heels.

We stare at each other for one sizzling moment before slamming together, mouths fused, hands grabbing, crazed for each other. The intensity is like nothing I've ever felt before. I crave him like my next breath. We tumble onto the bed, a tangle of arms and legs. He rolls on top of me, taking his weight on his forearms, kissing me roughly. I spear my fingers through his thick hair, overwhelmed by all that I'm feeling. There's nothing but the heat of his body, the fire igniting between us, his taste, his scent. He shifts, kissing his way down my throat, across my collarbones, his tongue dipping to the hollow between them.

"My turn," I tell him, pushing at his shoulders. "I've been wanting to lick every spectacular muscular ridge on you since the first time we met."

He rolls off me, onto his back, and holds his arms out to his sides. "Have at it."

I straddle him, victorious, my hands on his shoulders, taking in his magnificent chest.

"Well?" he teases. "Just going to look at me?"

I lean down and kiss him, sinking my teeth into his full lower lip and then sucking it. He groans. My hands roam from his square jaw down his neck and over the swell of his shoulders. His hands grip my hips, but they're not moving. I shift lower, kissing and nipping and tasting my way down, stopping to flick my tongue over his flat nipple. He moans, and I smile. I keep going, exploring his abs, running my tongue along them, and along the sides, his musky scent exciting me further. I shift, taking his massive erection in hand and running my tongue along the length of it. He groans long and low. I lick the salty drop off the tip and draw him into my mouth. His fingers tangle in my hair as his hips lift off the mattress. I take him as deep as I can, lifting my gaze to his gorgeous face. His jaw is slack, his eyes soft, watching me. I keep going, wanting to give to him after he's given so much to me. I'm damp between the legs, achy with need, his pleasure adding to mine.

He jerks and gives my hair a sharp tug. "Ruby!"

I reluctantly loosen my hold and lift my head. "What?"

"My turn," he growls.

My eyes widen at the roughness that's new to his voice, and then he's on me, his mouth sealed over mine as he lowers me under him. I wrap my arms around his neck and open my legs, cradling him.

He kisses a trail to my ear. "Jesus. So wet. I haven't even touched you yet."

"I got excited sucking you off."

He drops his head for a moment.

"Phillip?"

He lifts his head, holds my jaw with one hand, and kisses me. "So fucking sexy." He kisses me again, long and deep, his hand cupping my breast, caressing it, and then he shifts, his mouth closing over it, drawing my nipple deep into his mouth, the hollows of his cheekbones pronounced. Pleasure spears through me, my womb aching with each sharp suck. My legs fall open, aching for him there. He shifts to the other breast, caressing, kissing, sucking. His teeth clamp over my nipple and I suck in air, my back arching, and then he gentles, licking my hard nipple and then suckling again. My breath is coming harder now, need clawing at me.

"Phillip, kiss me, fuck me." I want his mouth back up here, and I want him inside me.

He shifts lower suddenly and kisses my sex. I jolt. His warm blue-green eyes meet mine as he strokes me lazily with his fingers. "So sensitive," he croons.

"You surprised—ah!" My hips arch up, white-hot pleasure stealing my breath. He lowered his head and sucked just as his fingers thrust inside me. He's not taking his time with me now. He anchors my hip down with one hand while his fingers continue to thrust and stroke as his lips and tongue devour me. I'm trembling under him, my nails digging into his shoulders, whimpering incoherently, my brain screaming for release. I can't form the words. *I need, I need, please, please, please.*

He lifts his head, watching my expression as he works me with his fingers. I'm panting, jaw slack, flushed with heat. I still can't speak. He smirks, a very satisfied-looking smirk, and lowers his head again. *Yes!* Except now he's gentle, soft kisses, slow licks, his fingers gentler too.

I moan and tug his hair. "I'm so fucking close. Don't stop."

"I'm not stopping."

"More, more, more." I am shameless.

"Demanding little minx," he growls and proceeds to drive me out of my mind. He amps me up again and I'm so grateful I can't stop moaning. I'm loud, I don't care. His mouth, his beautiful hungry mouth, consumes me; his fingers own me. I'm so far gone, within minutes I'm shaking with need. My insides coil tight.

"Look at me," he says gruffly.

My eyes fly open, locked on his. He watches me as he lowers his head again, sucking gently, his fingers, oh, god, the pressure. My world goes dark for a moment and then it explodes, my hips bucking helplessly against him. Electric sensations surge through my body, radiating out from my core to the tips of my toes; even my scalp is tingling. I'm a shimmering shooting star flying through the heavens.

He climbs up my body, strokes my sweaty hair back, and gives me a kiss. I smile against his lips. I'm limp, melting into the mattress. I vaguely think I should invite him to fuck me now, but I can't speak, can't move. He doesn't seem to mind. He lies on his side next to me and runs his hand over me, stroking me from shoulder to wrist, down my side, my hip. Even this feels good, warm sensations radiating everywhere he touches.

Finally, I find my voice. "I want to do more, but I can't seem to move."

"Shh, just let me touch you."

So I do. I lie there warm and relaxed while he runs his hands over me, until he finally pulls me into his arms and just holds me. I snuggle into his heat, safe and content and satisfied. The truth slams into me—

I am in love.

Fuck. No. This is supposed to be our one night in Paris, our bubble, our memory. Tears sting my eyes. Dammit.

I grab his head and kiss him hard, thrusting my tongue in his mouth, desperate to get back to passion and raw need. He's right there with me, his mouth demanding, and then he rolls on top of me, fitting himself between my legs. He stills suddenly and turns to the nightstand. He's left a condom there. I didn't even see him do that.

He rolls it on and then settles between my legs, his big hand cradling my face, gazing into my eyes.

Emotion clogs my throat, and I swallow hard.

"You okay?" he asks.

I grab his ass and pull him close. "Yes, fuck me."

He thrusts hard, taking me to the hilt, his mouth sealing over mine, swallowing my soft cry. He's so much bigger than me. He's stretching me, thick and hard, bringing a deep ache. He shifts to whisper in my ear, "You're so tight. So good."

I try to relax under him. And then he kisses me tenderly as he pumps into me, slow and sure, and I do relax again. The pleasure builds slowly.

He gazes down at me with a look of such tenderness I'm momentarily breathless. No man has ever looked at me like this when we're fucking. Because it's not fucking, he's making love to me.

I rake my nails down his back and bite his neck. His reaction is swift and sure, his hand sliding under my hip, lifting me for deeper penetration as he pounds into me, his breath harsh by my ear.

"Come with me," he rasps.

"Yes," I gasp out. I'm close, and he's relentless, pushing me closer and closer to the edge. My body clenches around him, my breathing ragged.

He holds my jaw, our gazes lock, our breaths merge as our bodies merge. His voice is deep and commanding. "Now."

I break, the orgasm ripping through me. He lets go, thrusting through my release, bringing more and more pleasure, wave after wave, until we're both spent. He gives me his weight, a delicious feeling. I try to memorize everything about this moment. The musky scent of sex, our heated skin pressed together, the pounding of my heart, the euphoric high.

It is a *perfect* moment.

He eases his weight off, holding himself over me as he

cradles my jaw and kisses me. "Rest now. I've got plans for you."

I'm too sated to move, the words form slowly in my dreamy state. "Should I be concerned?"

His eyes are warm on mine. "Only if multiple orgasms concern you."

I smile what I'm sure is a goofy wide smile. "I think I lo—" I clamp my mouth shut.

He stills. I stare at his chin, unable to meet his eyes, desperately wishing I could take it back.

He rolls off me and out of bed.

I scrunch my eyes shut tight, berating myself for blurting what is probably just emotional stuff coming up because I haven't been with anyone since my ex. I scared him off. *Nice going, Ruby. You and your bubble. Oh, sure, we'll be casual, only a happy memory.*

The music shuts off abruptly. The silence stark. *Party's over.* I thought we'd stay the night, but I ruined it. Now it's one and done.

I sit up, thinking I should get dressed. Obviously I suck at this casual thing. But wait—

Phillip is coming back to me. He's naked, gloriously proudly naked, carrying the champagne and chocolate, two fluted glasses dangling between the fingers of one hand.

My eyes water, and I press my lips tightly together. He's not leaving. I didn't ruin everything.

He sets everything on the nightstand. Then he drags the covers onto the bottom of the bed, nudges me flat on my back, and pulls them over me too. He joins me without a word.

I remain lying on my back, mouth clamped shut,

unsure what to say, if anything. Should I pretend I didn't almost blurt out the *L* word?

He's on his back next to me and shifts to his side, facing me. "Ruby."

"Hmm?"

"Finish your sentence."

I gulp and stare at the ceiling. "What sentence?"

His warm hand slides to my stomach. "You know which sentence."

I consider my options—denial, compliance—and the potential consequences. My tender heart needs protection. I'm such an idiot for thinking I could do casual. Now my heart's swinging in the wind. "Why?"

"I want to hear it."

I can't go there. It's too risky. "It was just a reaction in the moment. I didn't mean anything by it."

His hand slides up my ribs. "Just the orgasm speaking?"

I laugh a little. "Yeah."

"I see." He pulls me into his arms, chest to chest, and tucks my head under his chin, cupping my head with one hand. He lets out a breath and murmurs, "I hope it will speak again because…I think I do too."

I can't breathe. He's in love with me too. My heart races. How did we get here so fast? And what am I supposed to do with this incredible gift?

10

———

Phillip

I lie in the dark, holding Ruby, who fits in my arms perfectly, my mind turning over next steps. I can't help but think—despite the terrible timing, despite both our baggage—that this is a good thing. She has strong feelings for me, and I've been trying to deny mine, but it's no use. I already thought we were compatible, but now that we've finally crossed the line, I know we are, in every important way. She was made for me, my soul mate. She doesn't care about my title, my wealth, my stupid royal hottie moniker. She sees the real me. Unlike my previous girlfriends, she doesn't have a vain, shallow bone in her body. She's warm, honest, open, a bright bundle of energy that I want to keep close. The moment I stopped looking for her, she came into my life.

I breathe her in, the soft floral scent of her shampoo and something sweet that's distinctly Ruby. She rolls to her other side with a soft sigh. She's sleeping. I spoon her from behind, turned on by the contact but also sleepy. My mind drifts and I close my eyes.

I must've fallen asleep. I wake with one hand on her breast and the other between her legs. She's hot and wet.

"Are you awake?" I ask, mildly alarmed I was messing with her while she slept.

She whispers over her shoulder, "Yeah. I put your hands where I needed them, hoping you'd wake up and get the hint."

I smile. *Get the hint.* She is definitely made for me—playful, sexy, and fun. "Hang on." I grab another condom from where I stashed them earlier, roll it on, and spoon her again, except this time I thrust inside her. I hear her sharp intake of breath. She's petite, tight, and in this position, even tighter. She feels fucking amazing. I open her leg wide and pull it back to rest over mine; then I slide my hand right back where she wanted it, stroking her rapidly. She arches back into me as if to escape my fingers, but I've got her caught, pushing her hard to the edge as I slowly pump into her. I loved making her break earlier, a complete shuddering surrender that made my inner caveman roar in triumph. I didn't know I needed that until she gave it to me.

She reaches back, her nails digging into my shoulders, her back arched, soft cries escaping that make me thicker and harder. I force myself to pump slow, wanting to prolong it for her.

"Phillip!"

I soften my touch and she goes limp, her nails releasing their hold, her back relaxing against me. Her response to my touch is intense. It consumes her just as it does me.

I kiss along her neck, the satin skin hot to the touch. She angles her head to give me better access. I slide my hand up her flat stomach to her soft breast, cupping it, and then shift, clamping my fingers on her nipple. She jolts, and I release her nipple, sliding my hand back to pleasure central as I thrust steadily inside her, slow and deep. Then I keep my hand still, cupping her between the legs as I let the feeling build inside me. She feels incredible, tight and hot, and it takes every ounce of willpower to hold back.

She arches back into me over and over, taking me deeper, her breath coming in short pants. Then she grabs my hand and makes my fingers stroke her.

I thrust deep, holding her tight to me, and give her neck a nip. "Tell me what you want."

"Your fingers," she gasps out. "I swear you know when I'm close and you're toying with me!"

I strum her lightly with my thumb, and her breath shudders out. "You're so much fun to play with I can't help but toy with you."

She growls in frustration, and I give her a little more. She whimpers, and I give her even more, my touch firmer, my thrusts faster. She arches back against me, her hand reaching back and gripping my hair.

"You'll come when I let you," I whisper in her ear. She shivers, and I clamp her still, cupping her between the legs firmly, my cock buried deep inside. She moans softly and relaxes into me, a surrender. A vision of tying her up flashes through my mind, and I surge deep, thrusting over and over. *Fuck, fuck, fuck. Hang on.* I need her with me.

I stroke her softly, allowing myself another deep thrust. Her moans turn to a keening sound that fills my ears like a roar. Her body clamps down around me, and I give her what she needs, sending her over the edge. She breaks on a harsh cry, her body shuddering around me. I pump hard and deep, racing toward my own release, her soft cries spurring me on, and then I let go, the climax slamming hard in a rush of pleasure. I hold her tight to me, my body racked with it, still pumping, the sensation incredible. Finally I still, holding her in my arms.

We're both breathing hard, our bodies slick with sweat. She goes limp. That means I did my job right.

I stroke her hair back from her face and smooth it over her shoulder.

She hums a happy sound. "Phillip?"

I stroke her hair again, loving the silky feel of it. "What is it? Let me guess, you want to thank me for a thoroughly satisfying fuck."

She turns to look at me over her shoulder, her eyes heavy-lidded. "I am so getting you back." She flops onto the mattress on her stomach.

I grin and caress the sweet curve of her bottom. "I look forward to it."

No response. I think I wore her out again.

~

Ruby

Is it wrong that I invited Phillip into the bath and then teased him mercilessly, rubbing against him, stroking him, and then asking him to wash me before retreating to the other side of the tub? That is called payback, people, and no one deserved it more than him. He gets off on holding me hostage, milliseconds from orgasm, and then pulling me back to square one. So I've kept him at square one for nearly an hour now, and I am loving it. Hmm, maybe I get off on it too. Could we be better matched? A twinge of sadness pierces my happy bubble. I'm heading home soon, and he's going on a global tour for who knows how long? A year or more. We're so different, it doesn't make sense why we fit so well together.

"C'mere, Ruby," he croons from across the tub. "This champagne has your name on it."

I don't move because I suspect he's about to let loose his own form of payback. This is *my* party. His big hand clamps around my ankle and gives me a tug. Not hard enough to pull me under, just enough to nudge me. I ignore the hint and redo my hair in its messy updo with the hair band I found in my purse. His hand slides up my calf to my knee, pushing my leg open. A definite forward move in the sensual torture game.

"You're sneaky," I tell him, rapidly finishing my hair.

He grips my thigh and glides me through the water to him, bringing the champagne glass to my lips. I take a sip, and he takes a sip from it too, his aquamarine eyes intent on mine. I could drown in those eyes. All of me warms from throat to chest to belly just from one look.

I break eye contact and peer around him. "Where's the chocolate? We should have that with the champagne." It's the wee hours of the morning, around four a.m. last I checked. Chocolate sounds like a great early breakfast and I'm hungry.

He doesn't reply; instead he gives me more champagne, tipping the glass up for me to take a healthy swallow. I don't mind. It's delicious, better than any champagne I've ever had. He finishes the rest and sets the glass back on the tub's ledge.

He cradles my face with both hands. "I'm going to tell you something, and I don't want you to be mad."

I blink. Normally I'd tense for bad news, but it's impossible after soaking in this relaxing bath, getting multiple orgasms wrung out of me, and drinking champagne on an empty stomach. "What is it?"

A smile plays over his lips. "That wasn't a box of chocolate I had delivered. It was a box of condoms."

I splash him. "Phillip! I was looking forward to that chocolate!"

He laughs and wipes the water from his eyes. "You want me to order some chocolate?"

"God, no. They'd think we need more condoms."

"I'll be clear what we really want."

I flush, imagining that conversation. *No, not condoms this time, we're still putting those to good use, thanks. Yes, I want candy in the box.* "No, thanks."

"Okay."

I put my hands to my overheated cheeks. "I'm so embarrassed."

"You wanted me so badly. What was I supposed to do? Deny you your baser urges while I took a trip to the pharmacy?" He cups his hands over his mouth and announces, "Hallo, everyone! Prince Phillip Rourke is in need of a box of condoms!"

I laugh.

He grins. "I had to be discreet."

"Why didn't you tell me what it was?"

He cups the back of my neck and pulls me in for a quick kiss. "Because you were already jumpy about the guards being nearby, and I didn't want you even more jumpy knowing I asked the concierge to hide a dozen condoms in a chocolatier box. Yet another reason it's good you don't understand French. I can surprise you with thoughtful condom gifts."

"That was thoughtful." I beam at him. I can't help it. His consideration of my feelings is beyond what I thought any man was capable of. "Wait, you wouldn't use my ignorance of French against me, would you?"

He puts a hand to his heart. "You wound me. Now thank me for the condoms."

I climb into his lap and wrap my arms and legs around him. "Thank you."

He pushes my hair back behind my ear and cradles my jaw. "When you're with me, you have to get used to being in the public eye. And doing some things a little differently."

"Like order condoms disguised as chocolate."

He kisses me and smiles against my mouth. "Exactly."

And then I kiss him passionately, with everything I'm feeling for this wonderful man. There's only hunger and a need that grows more intense with every joining. I need this. I need him.

Hours later, I step out of the shower and wrap myself in a plush white towel. Phillip is still in the shower, his palms flat against the tile wall, his head hanging low as he catches his breath. I'm pretty pleased with my work there. This is a fun game. After our bath, we went back to the bed, made love, slept, made love again, and then hours later made it to the shower. I just gave him a blowjob he won't soon recover from. It was only fair after he asked me so politely to please allow him to tie me to the bedposts and then claimed control of my orgasms. I swear I blacked out after the fifth one.

I grab another towel and snap his ass with it. He straightens and narrows his eyes at me.

"Move it, Rourke. We need to get dressed so we can get something to eat."

He grabs the towel, wraps it around his waist, and steps into my personal space. "You are high on power."

I grin. "I am. You have only yourself to blame. You taught me the game."

He wraps my hair around his fist and gives a tug, tilting my face up for his kiss. "I fucking love it." Only it sounds like *I love you.* Fierce, intense, heartfelt.

I stare at him, searching his features, my heartbeat pounding in my ears. Neither of us has actually said it full out. It terrifies and elates me at the same time.

He gazes down at me steadily. "Come with me on the Global Sun Water tour."

I swallow down the lump of emotion. "Phillip, I know we've had a wonderful night together, but we agreed on a limit."

"It's only five weeks."

"I need to get home."

He drops his grip on my hair, and I step out of the steamy bathroom, searching for my clothes, which I haven't worn since we stepped into this oasis of a hotel room.

He watches me for a moment and then turns from me, gathering his clothes. We dress in silence.

Back to reality.

He orders us lunch from room service. It's awkward now. I wring my hands together, hating that it's gotten to this point after all the fun and, yes, real affection between us.

"I'm going to check in with the guards," he says and leaves.

I wander to the window, not really seeing anything,

suddenly exhausted. I slept only in short intervals last night. Somehow I know a long night's sleep won't be enough to ease the heaviness in my limbs. I have to go home. I have a chance at a real career waiting for me there. My baby sister will be here soon. My career and family are important to me. And I don't kid myself that five weeks more with Phillip will be easy to walk away from. I'm falling for him and I'll only get in deeper. That doesn't mean I'll get commitment back from him either. All I'll get is hurt. And I'm not ready to go to that dark place again.

I did the right thing turning him down. My gut knots, and I take a deep shuddering breath. No matter how shitty it feels right now, the answer has to be no.

Phillip returns a few minutes later. He takes my hand and guides me to the sofa, sitting next to me. "Hear me out. I'm only asking for five weeks of your time. Go with me just for the tour with Global Sun Water. All expenses paid. No strings. Then you can go back home and I'll start my work for the UN."

I close my eyes for a moment, torn by the earnest sincerity in his voice. It's so much easier to say no when I'm not looking at him. I remind myself there's no way that we could extend our time together without a lot more risk to both of our hearts. It'll only prolong the inevitable breakup. I hazard a glance at him. His eyes are intent on mine, his expression hopeful.

I blow out a breath. "Phillip, my career is just starting to get back on track. I've got sixteen of Anna's friends who want me to do a consultation at their homes for them. It will be the first time I've ever been an entrepreneur, and I could be a success at it. After the low point I hit, it would mean so much to prove myself. And you know I've got a baby sister on the way. I want to be part of her life, a big part. I need to go home." I leave out the part about the inevitable heartbreak. My heart is already breaking just knowing this is our goodbye.

"Your new clients can wait five weeks, and your sister won't be here for four more months. We could have more of this incredible experience together. You enjoyed your-self, right?"

Maybe I misread his intentions. Here I am wallowing in deep emotions while he sees it as an extended Paris for us, casual and fun. I wish I could just enjoy the moment like he does. Even so, letting myself enjoy the moment, agreeing to five more weeks, will change me. I'll fall one hundred percent. It will be impossible to protect my heart. The risk is too great. I can't see how this would work between us long-term with our very different lives, assuming he actually wants a committed relationship. Not at all a sure thing.

"Phillip—"

"Just answer the question." He cups my jaw, his finger stroking the sensitive spot under my ear, drawing a shiver. "Did you enjoy yourself?"

"Yes," I breathe. I can't resist his touch, can't help but melt.

He flashes a smile. "So let's keep it going. Why turn away from a good thing?"

I swallow hard, forcing myself to ask, "You mean this would be our Global Sun Water bubble?" I need to know where he stands—casual fun or something more.

He leans close, looking deep into my eyes. "No more bubble. This is you and me. I know the timing is bad with us both heading in different directions. I know you have a life back home. But, Ruby, I have feelings, deep feelings, and, if you do too, I think we should give it a chance. Just a little more time."

My heart thunders in my chest, scared yet hopeful. I'm not alone in the deep waters. Maybe, just maybe, it's a risk worth taking. "And then what?"

He carefully tucks a lock of hair behind my ear, the gentle gesture undoing me. "We'll cross that bridge when we come to it. Let's just enjoy the moment. Can you do that?"

I bite my lip, my eyes stinging with unshed tears. I so want to enjoy the moment because it means I can have him. "I need some time." I stand. "I'm going to take a walk. Clear my head."

"But lunch is on its way."

"I'll grab something when I'm out."

He pulls out his wallet and hands me some bills. "I'll be here. Take as long as you need. Call me if you get lost."

I take the cash. I still only have US bills. "Thanks."

I grab my coat and purse and rush out the door. The guards nod at me, but otherwise don't seem surprised by my sudden departure. I don't know if they were listening or if all of Phillip's women take off after their night together. *Stop that. He cares for you.*

I need food first to think clearly. I stop at a small patisserie and get myself a chocolate croissant and coffee. It's exactly what I need, the croissant buttery and sweet, the caffeine waking me up.

I take a look around and head toward a park in the distance. Once there, I walk every path there is and then reverse it, until finally I stop and take a seat on a bench. If I go home—back to my family and building my business—it means I leave Phillip behind forever. My throat tightens. I'm already in deep enough to know that will be hard. I'll catch glimpses of him in the news as he does his charitable work, lending his name and warm personal touch to a great cause. Paris and our time on Villroy will be a precious bittersweet memory. But if I travel with him for five weeks on the Global Sun Water tour, building more memories with him, it ultimately ends in the same place, me going home without him.

Either way, I have Phillip as a precious bittersweet memory.

Either way, I end up alone.

Either way, I love him.

I do. It's too late to protect my heart. The only question is, would anything change in those five weeks that could possibly mean I don't end up alone? Is it, as Phillip said, worth the risk to give us a chance? Is there some way we could have a future together?

He's going to be the freaking UN Ambassador for Clean Water, traveling wherever they need him. I have a life in Tampa. He'd be wasted there. He belongs on the world stage, and I would just be background, an appendage to his work. I want something for myself. Where is the common ground?

It's just five weeks, a voice in my head whispers. *Take what happiness you can.*

I slowly get to my feet. I want to be happy.

I want Phillip.

That's all that matters. What we have is special. I will enjoy the moment because moments are all we have. Nothing in life is a sure thing, and love is worth the risk.

I turn and walk briskly back to the hotel, my heart racing, cheeks flushed, a lightness to my step. I realize suddenly I'm smiling. I hurry through the lobby, back to our suite, and knock on the door. "It's Ruby." I don't have the key.

Rafe's voice barks behind me, "Ruby for you, sir."

Guard confirmation, check. The door opens and Phillip's gaze searches my face.

I step inside, the door shutting behind me. I throw my arms up, a beaming smile on my face. "Yes!"

"Ruby." That one word is filled with so much— warmth, gratitude, happiness. He pulls me into his arms, and I melt against him, wrapping my arms around his waist and settling my cheek on his chest, a deep sense of contentment filling me. This is our moment and it is perfect. I have no doubt that he cares for me as much as I do him. I won't think of the future. I have to enjoy the now.

He kisses the top of my head. "I have a good feeling about this. Thank you."

I look up at him and work to keep it light. "Don't thank me. You'll probably get sick of me." *We'll probably wreck each other.* I ruthlessly push that fear down. Here and now is all that matters. I can't believe I'm doing this. It's like the adrenaline rush as the roller-coaster car lurches bit by bit up the towering hill, knowing there's a plunge ahead. *I'm plunging, baby!*

"I could never get sick of you." He hugs me tight and my entire body relaxes. How can I be scared when I feel so right in his arms?

He straightens. "There will be a lot of press. I won't deny it will help me reputation-wise to be seen with you for a steady five weeks after all that royal hottie business. Would you mind if we let people believe we have a committed relationship?"

I nod, already liking where this is going. "I'm happy to

restore your rep. What would I have to do? Pretend we're engaged or something?"

"No. You don't have to lie. Just look at me adoringly, as you do." He winks, and I laugh a little. *Do I do that?* I should be embarrassed, but I enjoy him too much to pretend otherwise. "The press and gossips will put together their own version of events. It'll look good that you and I are seen together doing great work for the entirety of my five-week tour."

"Wow. Me on a global tour. Pretty cool."

He grimaces. "It's not a vacation kind of trip. Some of the places are rough, but the people are wonderful."

"Where are we going?"

"Africa, Southwest Asia, the Middle East, and India."

Whoa. "Did you know that my trip to Villroy was the first time I ever left the US?"

"No. How do you like travelling with me so far?"

"I love it."

He smiles, his eyes so warm on mine I can feel the love. All of me lights up, inside and out, my heart filled to bursting. I slowly lean in and kiss him. Another perfect moment. I'll collect them like pearls on a necklace and treasure them for the beautiful gift they are. Moment by moment, pearl by pearl, no one can take that away from me.

11

———————

Phillip

We return to the palace on Saturday in time to join Anna, Gabriel, and her guests for dinner in the formal dining room. We were delayed in Paris because I needed to get Ruby to a doctor for a yellow fever vaccination and health clearance. I'm hoping when Ruby sees the important work I'm doing with Global Sun Water, she'll join the cause and accompany me on the next journey working for the UN on behalf of clean water. It will become our mutual calling. I know she wants to "prove herself" in her career, but there's just no comparison between decorating and bringing clean water to people who desperately need it. My work is more important, and it can be her work too. We'll fit in visits to family. She'll want for nothing. I exhale sharply. I'm getting ahead of myself because—

I love her.

I know it, and I'm sure she knows it too. I'm done fighting it, done worrying about the risks. It's simply a fact. Somehow my inability to commit doesn't factor with her. She fits so easily, so naturally with me. I'm truly happy for the first time in a long while. I'm all in, and I'll do my best to get her on board. Anna will simply have to get used to it. Honestly, once we left Villroy, I was too caught up in Ruby to give Anna's warning to keep my hands off Ruby any thought at all. It doesn't matter. I love Ruby and I would never hurt her.

I guide her to a chair near where Anna will be sitting at the head of the table with Gabriel, and pull it out for her. Anna and Gabriel will arrive shortly. Anna's friends are filtering in, talking excitedly.

Ruby looks up at me adoringly. I don't need the words when it's written all over her beautiful face. She loves me.

"Thank you," she says, taking the offered seat. "Prince training school must include primo lessons on manners."

I laugh and take the seat next to her. "And so much more."

She leans close and kisses me. "Don't I know it."

"Omigod!" a woman screeches. "You two are together? That must've been some date!"

It's the black-haired woman who bid outrageously on me. "Yes, we're together," I tell her. "I'm sorry, I've forgotten your name."

"Mindy."

"Thank you for your bid, Mindy. All of this was for a great cause. I know Anna is pleased."

She nods and turns to Ruby. "Did he really take you to Paris?"

Ruby smiles tightly. "Yes. Dinner in Paris. And Phillip played tour guide."

"Wow. The other princes stayed local. Picnic on the beach, private dinner in the royal dining room, that kind of thing. You got lucky."

"Yes. Well." Ruby flushes bright pink and looks to me like *help me out here.*

I smile at Mindy. "Ruby was here early to lend a hand with the guest suite. We've gotten to know each other well on her extended visit. That's why our date was a little more elaborate than the other auction dates."

Mindy nods. "Ruby, I'm so looking forward to your consultation. I just bought a house and it's practically a blank slate. I can't wait to have you work your magic on it."

"Absolutely!" Ruby says. "I'm looking forward to it too. I'll be back in Tampa in early November. About five weeks from now. Is that okay?"

Mindy frowns. "Bummer. I was really hoping to have some furniture before Thanksgiving. I'm hosting this year."

"I could help you by email, or, if you let me know what you like, maybe we could look over a few ideas before you leave."

"Not much time. I leave tomorrow."

"Sorry," Ruby says. "Please keep me in mind for when I return. I'm really looking forward to working with you." There's a hint of desperation in her voice.

"Sure," Mindy says with a tight smile.

Ruby immediately stands and visits with the other women, probably trying to lock down her new clients. She's smiling brightly, but I can tell she's tense. She's afraid to lose them. If she's with me, she won't need to work. I keep that to myself. She wants to prove herself, but there are other more important ways she can do that.

When she returns to her seat, I whisper to her, "Try not to come off as desperate. Better to look confident like you're already a success."

She bares her teeth at me and whispers, "I am desperate. I need the work."

A servant opens the dining room door and announces, "Their Majesties, King Gabriel and Queen Anna."

We all stand. I bow my head to them both and signal to Anna's friends, not used to royal protocol, to follow suit. Ruby bows her head and curtsies and the women catch on. Gabriel dressed for dinner in a light gray suit. Anna is in a sleeveless black dress that clings to her curvy body. Now that she's queen, she's declared exposed shoulders are fine for royal women, though she's bowed to the protocol to keep her cleavage covered after the gossips had a field day with a series of pictures of her in her revealing wardrobe. She agreed that wasn't the focus she wanted on Villroy's monarchy, even though she thought they were all repressed asses. She's first and foremost concerned with Villroy's future.

Gabriel walks at her side, his hand on the small of her back, guiding her toward their seats. As king and with royal bloodlines, his place is at the head of the table, hers adjacent to him.

He waits for her to take her seat before taking his. "Please have a seat," Gabriel says with a warm smile to the rest of us. "So nice to see you all."

Wow. Gabriel was never much of a smiler before Anna. It's great to see.

Anna beams. "Thank you all so much for coming all this way to help me and Gabriel with our passion project. It's because of you that we're able to move forward with the next phase, the day spa and natural beauty product line. And you're all invited back when it's complete for free spa treatments! I want you to be my very first guests!"

The women cheer and talk all at once.

"Thank you!"

"You're the best!"

"You rock, Anna!"

"Ha!" Anna says. "Don't thank me yet. You're secretly my guinea pigs. I know I can count on your honest opinion on everything. Plus you're all veterans of the spa experience."

The women are excited, except Ruby, who looks worried. Maybe she's still thinking of the potential loss of her new clients.

The servants bring in the first course and the women quiet down.

Anna is next to Ruby and leans past her to look at me. "Phillip, Ruby tells me you've been good to her. Keep it up, please."

"Yes, Your Majesty," I intone.

She laughs. "Okay, you can say it, I misjudged you. I'm happy so long as she's happy. And, Ruby, I'm so excited you get to go on this tour!" Ruby called ahead to let Anna know about the change in travel plans, and I guess she shared about our relationship too. I have a relationship. It doesn't hold that charge of horror it used to. Instead it just feels incredibly amazing.

"I'm excited about the tour." Ruby lowers her voice, and I lean close to listen. "I'm a little worried that when I get home, I won't have any career to speak of. I've been really excited about all the new clients. So far, your friends aren't too keen on waiting. I understand. They're excited, and by the time I get back, it's close to the holidays— Thanksgiving, Christmas, and New Year. They don't want their homes to be in upheaval while trying to enjoy the holidays, so it just means a longer wait."

Anna sends me a pointed look. I'm not sure what she

wants me to say, so I just speak from the heart. "You're worth waiting for, Ruby. They'll see."

Ruby rolls her eyes and whispers to me, "It's not that simple. Americans don't like to wait. They're used to instant gratification. They'll move on."

"Then you'll find other work."

Anna nods. "You'll land on your feet, Ruby. I'd love to offer you a job, but I'm afraid it'll be a while before we get to the point where we need interior design again."

"And I'll help you find work," I tell her. "Better work."

Her brows scrunch together. "What do you mean better work?"

I hesitate. I don't want to flat out say her work isn't important, but, in the grand scheme of things, it's not. I keep my voice low. "No one's career was ruined by waiting five weeks."

She opens her mouth and then shuts it. "This isn't the right place to talk."

"Agreed."

She stabs a shrimp in her shrimp cocktail. "But I'm not sure you understand about careers, being a prince."

Anna widens her eyes and turns to talk to Gabriel. Ruby *was* a little snippy. I'm not going to fight with her. She'll see the right path soon enough.

I move on to more pressing matters with Ruby. "Tomorrow we'll go over the itinerary with the press secretary. He'll be accompanying us, along with security and my valet. Would you like a maid to attend to you?"

"I'm fine on my own." Still snippy.

I try for a joking tone. "Is it because your maid has a crush on me and you're overcome by jealousy?"

She gives me a sideways look and I grin. She shakes her head, smiling. "Big head."

"I need it for these big shoulders."

Anna catches my eye and smiles at me. It gives me a boost to know she approves of the match after telling me to keep my distance earlier. Ruby will already have a close friend on the inside, which will make her transition to royal life easier. All I need to do is cement our relationship in these next five weeks. And that begins now.

I shift to whisper in her ear, "You'll be staying in my suite at the palace starting tonight."

She whispers back fiercely, "You could occasionally make your requests in the form of a question, *Your Highness*. Otherwise, you sound demanding, which is irritating to an independent-minded woman like myself. Just FYI." She never calls me Your Highness, not even from the first moment we met when it would've been proper. She must really be pissed about all this potential client business.

"But it's not a question," I inform her. "It's a fact."

"Would you like to stay in my suite?" she asks.

"No, darling. You're staying in my suite."

She studies me. "I can't tell if you're being deliberately obtuse or you're so used to getting what you want that you don't know any other way to be."

I dig into my shrimp cocktail. They both sound bad. Also, it was the first thing. I can be very accommodating, but not with her. Not until I cement this thing between us. After we're a definite thing, I'll give her anything she wants as long as she's by my side.

She leans close. "I'll generously say you're being obtuse on purpose because you want me that bad. Mostly because it makes me feel good to think it. If you turn out to be a demanding a-hole, well, that's not gonna fly with me."

I shake my head. "Once again you wound me, Ruby. Now thank me for the kind invitation."

Her head whips toward me. I force a straight face, and she cracks up. She can't stay mad at me because she loves me.

"You offer so many things to give thanks for," she says with a smile.

"I'm very princely that way."

She leans against my side for a moment, pressing her shoulder against my arm before straightening and taking a drink of wine.

"I got us another box of chocolates."

She chokes on her wine, and I pat her back. She knows what I really mean.

"Five, actually," I add. "It's a long trip."

"Okay over there?" Anna asks us.

I nod. "She's fine. Just went down the wrong pipe."

Ruby holds up a finger while she coughs. Finally she calms down, wipes her eyes, and tells Anna, "Your brother-in-law has a wicked sense of humor."

"Does he, now?" Anna asks, resting her chin on her hand. "What's so funny?"

Ruby turns to me. I keep my mouth shut. I'm not sharing that.

"Ooh, it's dirty," Anna says, turning to Gabriel. "They've got dirty jokes."

"Parlor," Gabriel says sternly.

I'm not sure what that means. He wants her to join him in the parlor? A hint at parlor manners?

Anna reaches under the table, and Gabriel jumps. "You okay, honey?" she asks. "Did a gator sneak up on you?"

Ruby laughs. "We have a lot of alligators in Florida.

Always have to be careful not to leave small dogs out in the yard or the gator will sneak up and eat 'em."

Gabriel glowers at Anna. She smiles back sweetly.

She's perfect for him. Just like Ruby is perfect for me. All I have to do is make it clear that our lives can work toward a greater calling together.

Ruby

Our first stop is Tanzania. We're fortunate to take the private jet, so the travel part is not a slog at all. First we meet up with the Global Sun Water people, who are from England. Their NGO started from a university's engineering department. Phillip greets them warmly and introduces me as his "girlfriend and supporter of the cause." I'm immediately welcomed in. They need all hands on deck. We'll be visiting villages where solar water pumps were previously installed to check on them and perform repairs where needed, along with villages getting a pump for the first time. They explain that they've trained locals on maintenance, but it's not always easy to get parts delivered. Many parts are stolen before they reach their destination.

Before the trip to the village, I go with Phillip to meet the president of Tanzania and some important people in his administration. We have a formal lunch and Phillip appears to be in his element. I do my best to blend and take his lead on manners and proper greetings. But it's not until we reach the first village after a long journey in a Jeep through dusty hot savannahs that I see Phillip step out from behind the prince persona. It's a revelation.

Children race toward our Jeep as we approach the

village, and Phillip smiles and waves at them. We park and the guards, Henry and Rafe, exit first, urging the children back. The adults in the village hang back watching us. There's a large open shelter and several homes with no doors or windows, just a roof overhead. In the distance, the sun shines off the solar panels powering the water pump.

Phillip steps out of the Jeep, helps me out, and then urges Rafe back in a low command before greeting the children. "Hello! How's everyone doing?" He reaches out both hands and the children rush to high-five him. He's done this before, probably taught them the high five too. "This pretty lady is Ruby. Say hi, Ruby!"

"Hi, Ruby!" the children chorus.

"Hi, everyone." I smile and wave. I'm already drenched in sweat, even wearing a linen dress, hat, and sandals. Phillip is sweating too in his linen shirt and pants.

Phillip smiles at me and then looks toward a small figure in the shade of the shelter's porch. "David!" He turns to me. "Come meet David." He strides over to the shelter, where a young boy in a wheelchair waits. The boy smiles shyly. He's probably five or six. His legs end at the knees.

Phillip drops to his haunches so they're eye to eye. "So good to see you again, David. I brought my friend Ruby."

David smiles at me and turns to Phillip. "I can read a chapter. I've been practicing."

"Well, let's hear it. Have you got the tablet with you?"

David nods and points behind him.

Phillip stands and checks the pouch on the back of the wheelchair, pulling a digital tablet out. He hands it over to David and drops to one knee to listen, his head bowed toward the ground.

David presses a few buttons and begins to read about a mischievous puppy. It's painfully slow and he stops a few times in the beginning, stuttering over a tough word. Phillip lifts his head once David sounds confident, listening in rapt attention, occasionally nodding to encourage him.

Finally David finishes and puts the tablet down on his lap.

"Brilliant!" Phillip exclaims. "Very impressive. I wasn't reading that well until I was six and you're only five."

David beams.

"Keep at it," Phillip says. "Remember what we talked about. Education means opportunity, and what does opportunity mean?"

"A good job," David says.

"That's right. You want to see the pump's guts? We're going to tinker with it."

"Yeah!" David exclaims.

Phillip tucks the tablet back in the pouch and pushes him toward the pump, inclining his head for me to join them. More kids gather round to watch, only now they're carrying their own tablets and telling Phillip what they're learning with them.

I hang back, watching as Phillip talks to the kids and some of the adults who are helping with maintenance on the pump. He makes each kid feel special. My ovaries are bursting. He remembers a lot of their names, and he subtly keeps them out of the way of the workers. The press secretary snaps some pictures and urges me to get closer to Phillip.

I work my way through the crowd of admirers. Phillip turns to me. "Check out what Emmanuel's been doing online. He's already up to algebra. And he's ten!"

"Wow, that's great! So you're all learning online? Or do you go to school?"

"It's both," a woman says. "Hi, I'm Irene. I run the school, and now with the computers and tablets His Highness, Prince Phillip, has provided, we can go further, learning more online."

"That's wonderful." I turn to Phillip, and he smiles modestly. He never mentioned he was doing a technology-in-schools program.

"It is," Irene says enthusiastically. "And now the girls are in school as well."

My eyes widen. "They weren't before?"

She lowers her voice. "They were needed to fetch the water." She gestures toward the pump. "Now the machine does it, so they can go to school."

"I'm so glad to hear it," I say, though I'm a little stunned. It hadn't occurred to me girls couldn't attend school because they had to get water for their village. It's sexist and unfair, which angers me as a woman. At the same time, it's basic survival, which I have never had to contend with in my life. Probably everyone in the village has a specific role so they can all survive. My whole life I've taken for granted food, water, and shelter, even school. My world just shifted, my eyes open for the first time to the realities of a very different kind of life.

We leave an hour later, heading to another village. This next one will be getting a solar water pump for the first time.

I take my seat in the back of the Jeep with Phillip. He's waving bye to the kids, who are running alongside the car for a bit. Finally we're too far and the kids hang back.

"I didn't know the water was connected to education for girls," I tell him. "That blew my mind."

He nods. "It's one of the best benefits, beyond the basic need for water. Normally the villagers depend on the girls to walk every day to fetch water from far-off sources and carry it back in large heavy jugs. It takes several trips of backbreaking hard labor to get the needed water, which means they have no time for school. One of the other crucial benefits is the dramatic drop in waterborne diseases."

"And the educational technology part, was that your idea?"

He takes my hand. "It was a natural fit once I realized how water and education connected."

"And who funds that?"

"Me, at first, but I've managed to connect a few foundation grants with Global Sun Water's efforts."

"I'm sorry I said you had a big head before."

He smiles at me. "Maybe I do."

"What you have is a big heart." I put my hand over his heart. "You're amazing."

"Oh, well, now I really am going to get a big head."

"Don't joke. I'm being serious. This work you're doing is incredible, and your part in it is so impressive. I'm in awe."

He shakes his head. "Don't be. I'm mostly just a facilitator. But you see now why I feel so strongly about this work. It's become like a calling for me."

"Yes, I can see that."

"Good."

"Do you stay in a tent, or with one of the villagers as a guest in their home?"

He flashes a bright smile that lights up his face. "Is that what you thought? And you were still willing to spend five weeks with me, roughing it? Wow. And no. We stay in the closest city in a hotel. We're a visitor to their world. I don't want to impose on their resources. They'll feel obligated to offer food, which could mean some would go hungry."

I'm secretly glad we're going to be in a hotel and feel terribly guilty at the same time, knowing how far removed it is from their survivalist existence.

"Plus I need the security of a hotel with the guards," he says. "There are some who would put a ransom on me."

"Then I'm glad about the hotel."

He gives me a knowing look. "Changes your perspective, doesn't it? Makes you appreciate things more."

"Oh, yeah."

"I'm glad you're here, Ruby."

"Me too."

He lifts my hand and kisses the knuckles, his eyes intent on mine. I'm enthralled, feeling closer to him than ever before. Being so far from everything I know and having the welcome familiarity of Phillip by my side creates a deep intimacy. I don't know how I'm going to say goodbye to him. I'm not sure I can.

12

———

Ruby

Four weeks on the road with Phillip has been a whirl-wind of people and places. It's been eye-opening in more ways than one—seeing poverty up close at a level I previously didn't know existed, the resilience and surprising joy of the people we've met, the contrast in the disparity of wealth between the leaders of a country and their people. In each country, we've visited with heads of state, diplomats, and government leaders and been welcomed with fancy formal dinners and elaborate teas. We've also been welcomed in far-flung villages, slums, and rural farmland. Phillip surprised me with the ease he handles the different environments. What it's shown me is the kind of man he is deep down, a warm charismatic man who loves people, all people, no matter their station in life.

He remains affectionate, attentive, and considerate of me, making sure I'm comfortable wherever we land. No matter where we are during the day, at night we return to the best hotel in town. I'm not complaining. We've had many sexy nights together. I've even gotten used to sleeping with him. He's a spooner. I want to tell him I love him, but I can't seem to get the words out. He hasn't said it either. I can feel it, though. The love between us grows stronger every day.

In six days, we return to Villroy and I fly home the next day from there. That's the end for us, unless we attempt a long-distance relationship. I fear a year or more of distance would make us more miserable than a clean break. I'm not sure what to do. We have to have The Talk soon.

Now we're on our way back to the hotel in New Delhi, India, accompanied by Henry and Rafe, our constant security shadows. I still feel awkward talking freely to Phillip with two burly men sitting nearby, one in the backseat of the Mercedes with us, the other in the front seat. It's easier to forget about them when they're out of sight.

Phillip holds up his phone to me, showing me a picture of the two of us at last night's charity dinner on Global Sun Water's behalf. It was a black-tie event, and my elegant silk gown was provided by Phillip. He had me measured before we left Villroy, and the appropriate clothes for our itinerary were forwarded to our hotel at the first opportunity. He's a little like the fairy godfather to my Cinderella, not that I'd tell him that. Ha-ha. I don't think he'd like the comparison to a sparkly fairy.

"They love us together," he says. "They're calling us a power couple."

My stomach rolls. I'm not famous, rich, or powerful. That's all Phillip. My parents are beside themselves seeing me in the press with Phillip. I've kept in touch. They're proud of the charitable work I'm involved with and, at the same time, worried about my safety. The security guards only make them imagine terrible scenarios where they'll be needed. I've assured them I've never felt unsafe. My mom is dying to meet Phillip. She and I were both his fangirl followers when he was more fantasy man than reality. It's different, though, when you're the one caught up in the whirlwind of Phillip's life. I can't help but feel like an appendage to him, lost in his big shadow, and this power couple moniker doesn't sit well. It's a little too close to Phillip and Lana being dubbed the golden couple, part of the reason he was so into the relationship. I don't want or need others to comment on our relationship. He relishes it.

I turn to him. "I'm not really part of the power, but I'm glad you've gotten good press."

"Good? It's been fantastic! I may never be called the royal hottie again. Ruby, this is huge. And you are part of the power. They're calling us the power couple because our humanitarian efforts get results. I'm thrilled. It's pointing the spotlight where it's needed most." He squeezes my thigh. "We're a great team."

"I don't know how much credit I can take. I feel like I've just been along for the ride. This is your show."

He takes my hand, lifts it and brushes a kiss across my knuckles. His aquamarine eyes are warm and tender on mine. I melt like always. "It's ours. Together."

My throat tightens, and I press my lips together. "We need to talk."

A look of alarm crosses his face before he covers with a neutral expression. "When we get back to the room."

I nod and look out the window at the passing scenery. Downtown New Delhi, like many of the cities we've visited, is hot, fragrant, and crowded. We pass high-rise buildings and street-level shops, along with traffic, but the traffic here isn't just cars, it's pedicabs, taxis, bicycles, and pedestrians all crammed together on narrow streets. A man pushing a cart veers in front of our car, crossing the street. The slow pace gives me plenty of time to think on what the next step should be with Phillip. We've gotten close in a way we might not have been if we hadn't been traveling through so many foreign lands. He was the most familiar person to me when I often felt overwhelmed, either by the pomp and circumstance of high-level meetings or the abject poverty that tore at my heart. Through it all was Phillip, always warm and smiling, a steady familiar presence.

We're nearly at the hotel when he says excitedly, "I just got an email from the UN. They've seen all the good press around us and think together we can do a lot to draw attention to the cause." His eyes are intent on mine. "*Together*, Ruby."

I see his future with clarity in that moment and it is not my future. Traveling like this as a full-time job around the world, speaking at the UN and other foreign diplomatic meetings, giving interviews, drawing people together. That's what he's good at. And I would just be part of the background, not contributing in any way besides photo opportunities. I want to go home. I want to meet my baby sister, run my own business, be back in the country I love.

I blink back tears and look away. I can't break down here, can't have a heartfelt talk either, telling him goodbye. I have to hang on until we get to the privacy of our hotel room.

He cups my jaw, turning me toward him. "It's our shared press that's gotten me to this level. Ruby, come with me. This is our shared honor."

"I'm just background." My voice cracks.

He drops his hand and scowls. "You're much more than that."

I'm quiet. I don't want to disappoint him, but this is not my life.

He goes on in an urgent voice. "You've been connecting with the women in a way that I can't."

I shake my head, my voice strained by the tight lump of emotion caught in my throat. "They connect with you fine. They love you."

He frowns. "We'll talk more later."

The moment we're in the privacy of our hotel room, he takes my hand and guides me to the plush beige sofa in the palatial formal living room of our suite. We're staying at a hotel called Leela Palace, and it lives up to its name. I take some deep breaths, trying to calm the riot of emotions that erupted when I realized I have to tell him goodbye. I don't want to say goodbye.

He gives my hand a squeeze. "I thought you enjoyed your time on this tour. Why wouldn't you want to continue it?"

I hesitate, trying to figure out the best way to explain. "I have enjoyed myself, mostly because of you, but this isn't my thing. It's yours. My life is back in the US. My family, my new sister, building a career doing what I love."

"You won't be leaving your family forever. We can visit."

"It's not the same. I want to be a big part of my sister's life. I don't want to just pop in and out of it. And I'm starting a new business, which looks very promising, if I could just get back and follow up on all my new prospects."

"So you choose a job over a calling?"

I don't know what to say to that. Is one type of work more important than the other? I applaud his work, but I don't know that I want to be his helper. I want something of my own. And I do love interior design. There's no room for doing what I love in his future life. "I know it's hard to understand because what you're doing is so important, and I support it one hundred percent, but it's your calling not mine."

He stares at me. "I don't understand. I thought you believed in the cause."

"What about my job?"

His brows draw together. "Why do you persist in talking about your job? If you're with me, you don't have to work. After all we've seen on this trip, I'm sure you can see how important clean water efforts are. It raises the quality of life beyond mere survival. By comparison, decorating is meaningless, frivolous fluff."

I suck in air, my heart stopping for a moment and then lurching forward. All this time I thought he respected me and what I do. I cross my arms, hugging myself. "Well, it means something to me."

He stands and looks down at me. "I'm so disappointed in you. You're selling out for what? Money? Prestige? An ego boost?"

I leap to my feet. "I'm not selling out! I know this must be hard for you to understand since you never had to work a day in your life, but having a career I can be proud of means a lot to me. It's not selling out to want to take care of yourself."

He takes both my hands. "I'll take care of you. Stay by my side and you'll want for nothing. We'll continue on this important path together. Come with me to my meeting at the UN and let them know you want to be part of it."

I'm torn by the sincerity in his voice. I don't want to leave him, but I also don't want to give up what's important to me. I'll lose myself. Worse, he seems to want that, believing what I do is not worth a thing. But it is to me, and I know it brings joy to others. I won't allow myself to be his appendage, dependent on him for everything. That's just not how I'm made. I want, no, I *need* to stand on my own two feet.

He gives my hands a squeeze. "Don't underestimate the good PR we represent together. We're the power couple."

My shoulders slump. That seals it for me. I can feel myself retreating from him and this public world he lives for.

"Phillip, I care about you a lot." My voice breaks, choked with emotion, and I take a deep breath. "But this is your path, not mine. I don't want to be there just for PR and photo opportunities. Let's...how about this? We'll stay in touch, we'll visit whenever we can, and-and..."

He pulls away.

"I'll be cheering you on," I finish lamely. There's no easy way to merge our two paths, but I'm not ready to let go of him.

He crosses his arms and frowns. "Maybe I don't know you as well as I thought I did. I thought we were on the same page. Same values, same cause."

I don't know what to say. Maybe he's right. I can't make myself into whatever ideal image he had of me. I've been honest with him. His work is important, but it's not my work. And it's clear he doesn't value my work.

He goes to the balcony window and jerks the curtains open. The setting sun casts him in shadow, a proud regal figure, shoulders back, legs spread apart. He conquers whatever he sets his mind to. He has no idea what it is to struggle, to have to work hard, to need to achieve anything. Our two different worlds can never coexist. He belongs on the world stage, and I need to be grounded, working at what I'm good at, carving out my own niche in the world. And my family means everything to me. As an only child, I'm close with my parents, and I want to be close with my sister too.

I worry my lower lip. Phillip and I got so close on this trip too, living and working together. God, I hate the distance between us right now. "We still have a week together."

He doesn't bother to turn around. "I think it would be best if you leave now."

I gasp, my stomach dropping. "That's it? We're done?"

He turns, his expression hard. "Do you expect me to pretend everything is good between us?"

"It could be. We still…we connected. I—"

"We're on two diverging paths," he says coolly. "Let's not make this any harder than it needs to be."

I stumble back, shocked at his dismissal.

He pulls out his phone. "You needn't look so stricken. This was your choice. I asked you to join me; you declined."

I lift my chin, tears blurring my vision. "Then I'll go!" I wipe at my eyes, grab my purse, and rush to the bedroom, looking around for my suitcase.

Phillip appears in the doorway. "I'm calling my valet. He'll pack for you and accompany you to the airport."

"Don't bother!" I find the suitcase in the huge walk-in

closet and wheel it out, tossing it on the bed and unzip-ping it.

"I told you I'm taking care of it."

I hate how calm he is, like it means nothing to him that I'm leaving. Like we meant nothing at all! I grab my stuff from the dresser drawer in one big scoop and toss it in the suitcase.

He walks out of the bedroom, done with me and my annoying independence. No problem because I'm done with him and his demands. It's his way or no way. Forget that!

I empty the second drawer of clothes and cram every-thing in. The closet holds all the formal wear Phillip bought me, and I leave it all behind.

I head for the bathroom, grab my toiletry bag, and stuff everything inside it in a mad rush. I toss the bag in the suitcase, zip up the case, and wheel it to the living room, where Phillip is sitting on the sofa, looking at his phone.

"I'll pay for a cab and find my own way home," I tell him.

He doesn't reply.

"Bye," I snap.

Nothing.

His cold dismissal only fuels my need to escape. I whirl and rush through the door to the outside hallway, slamming face-first into the hard chest of a security guard. I look up into Rafe's glowering expression. "Move it. I'm going home."

"No, ma'am. It's not safe for you alone. Please wait inside for the necessary arrangements."

"Okay, okay." I turn back toward the door and then skirt left, taking off down the hall, my suitcase bumping along behind me. "Ah!" I yelp a moment later, restrained by arms of steel, my feet lifted right off the ground. It's Rafe, carrying me and depositing me back in the living room with Phillip. My suitcase follows a moment later. So humiliating.

"Don't try that again," Rafe growls before shutting the door.

I seethe.

Phillip shakes his head. "Impulsive, self-centered, money-centered. You are not the woman I thought you were."

I lose it, gesturing wildly. "You're exactly who I thought you were when we first met! Full of yourself and your press! You don't understand needing money or wanting to work hard because that's never been part of your life. If you want something, all you have to do is pick up the phone and the world drops at your feet."

He speaks into his phone, making arrangements and ignoring me.

I jab a finger at him. "See! You just proved my point!"

He punches the button to disconnect. His eyes are cold, his voice flat. "I won't deny I've been fortunate, but I resent you acting like that's all I am. I'm using my advantages to help the unfortunate."

I glare at him. "Make sure you order a really big halo!"

He glares back. "I'm providing clean water and education. All you do is add pretty wallpaper to a wealthy woman's master bath!"

I want to slap the self-righteous smug expression off his face. "Fuck you!"

He smirks. "We've done plenty of that, haven't we? Maybe that's where I went wrong, confusing sexual compatibility for any real-world compatibility."

I hate his haughty tone, like he's above me in every

way. "You're not better than me just because you do charitable work. Every contribution can be meaningful if it comes from the heart."

"Keep telling yourself that when you're picking out curtains. How heartfelt. How important."

I gasp. He's reduced me to insignificant. I am not insignificant! "How dare you condescend to me!"

There's a knock at the door.

Phillip shoots me a look of disgust before answering the door. We're joined a moment later by his valet, who bows to Phillip before heading to the bedroom. I follow him in to find him checking the dresser drawers for my things.

"I've already packed."

He moves to the closet.

"Leave the gowns. They're not mine."

"You might as well take them," Phillip says from behind me. "I doubt they'll fit anyone else. Small clothes for a small-minded person."

I whirl. "Go to hell."

He laughs, a mean laugh.

I've had enough. I will not engage with him any further. I turn away and tell the valet, "Leave them."

The valet takes my suitcase in hand. "Ma'am, when you're ready."

I nod and follow him out the door.

No goodbyes, nothing. Phillip and I are done.

I'm dry-eyed, filled with indignation at his callous treatment all the way to the airport. He's put me on a first-class nonstop to New York. I'll transfer from there back to my normal life in Tampa, back to my old bedroom in my parents' house, and start over, building my career with my new prospects. This was all a dream. Not my reality.

The flight attendant immediately fusses over me with a glass of champagne, warm nuts, a soft blanket, and a complimentary gift box, which I don't bother to open. All this luxury reminds me of the life I'm leaving behind with Phillip. I can't wait to get home and put all reminders of him behind me.

It isn't until the plane takes off that the tears come.

They don't stop for a very long time.

13

Phillip

My fury at Ruby lasted three solid days. I don't think anyone has ever made me more furious in my life. She chose a job over me, turned her back on what could have been an important path to take together. But when my fury fades, what's left is a deep grief that guts me. I can't eat, I can't sleep, I can barely focus on what I'm here to do. I can't even muster a smile for the people I meet in dire need of clean water. I drag myself through the days and finally cut it short a few days early, explaining to the Global Sun Water people that I'm ill and need to return home to recuperate.

I want to fix this thing with Ruby face-to-face, but I have to stop home first for Gabriel and Anna. They need the jet for a trip to Tampa, where Anna and Ruby are from. It's the fastest most direct way to get them there. Anna's foster father, Mike, who's been very ill from lung cancer, is asking for her.

The jet is being refueled and going through safety checks in France, so I have time to stop at home. The yacht is waiting to get me there fast. I meet up with Gabriel and Anna at the palace, where Gabriel is pacing outside their suite in the west wing.

"How is she?" I ask.

He jams a hand in his hair. "She insists on packing herself, but she's crying, and it's taking forever. She won't even let me help."

"I need to do for myself, Gabriel!" Anna hollers through the open door of their suite. "It's the one thing I can control."

I peek into the room. "Hi, Anna. I'm really sorry to hear about Mike."

"You're here!" She squashes her suitcase and zips it closed. "Let's go." She wheels her suitcase out.

Gabriel tries to take it from her, but she pulls it away. She rushes ahead of us toward the stairs. Gabriel signals for a servant to assist her.

"I'm going with you," I tell Gabriel. "Ruby is in Tampa now. I mucked things up and need to fix it."

He halts. "You're leaving too? I was going to put you in charge. I have a few duties to attend to and I need you to fill in. Fuck. Lucas?"

The royal duties fall in line with whoever is closest to the throne. Next in line after me is Lucas, the bachelor who caused a riot.

"Unless you want to ask Mother," I offer. "I'm sorry, but it's urgent I see Ruby."

He scowls. "You know our mother's in a delicate state right now." He stalks off, barking out a series of orders to some nearby footmen.

A short while later, we're all in the waiting Mercedes, the luggage being packed into the trunk, when Lucas knocks on the back window. Anna powers it down.

Lucas's eyes are sympathetic. "Take care, Anna. I'll be thinking of you and Mike."

She gives him a watery smile, reaches out, and squeezes his hand. "Thank you."

He turns to Gabriel and gives him a sharp salute before doing an about-face and marching back to the palace.

"Hopefully the palace will still be standing when I return," Gabriel mutters.

I can't worry about Lucas and what he might do. My mind is on what lies ahead. Gabriel is busy comforting Anna, who's subdued. I have plenty of time to think on our journey, and what I conclude is this—I need Ruby in my life. In all my excitement over making a contribution to the world, I forgot the most important thing. None of this means anything without love in my life. I should've started with that. I should've told her how much I love her. I hurt her. I wanted to hurt her and that was petty and wrong. She was right that I don't know what it's like to have career ambition. I've never had a job, never built a career. Maybe that's why my work on behalf of clean water became so important to me. For the first time in my life, I felt useful, needed, like what I did mattered. But none of that matters without her.

When we're on the jet, Anna takes a nap. Afterward, she takes the seat next to me. "Gabriel says its urgent you see Ruby to fix things between you. What happened?"

"I screwed up horribly."

"I'm sure it's not that bad. I know you have strong feelings for her. It's written all over your face."

I press my lips together for a moment, touched by her faith in me, however misplaced, and then I tell her everything, all the glorious highs and the really terrible low of our trip together.

"Damn, Phillip, were you *trying* to push her away?"

"No!" *Was I?* Did I sabotage it on purpose, still afraid of a real commitment because of Lana's betrayal? I'd hate to think that was the case. That can't be. I truly do love Ruby. Why didn't I tell her that? I'm such an idiot. I assumed way too much—that she knew I loved her, that she'd agree that my work was the best way for us to have a life together. I didn't even consider any other option.

"I didn't mean to push her away," I say miserably. "I was trying to pull her with me in a misguided stupid way."

"Really stupid. Do you think I would've stayed with Gabriel if he told me my job as a hairdresser was meaningless and insignificant? Or if he looked down on the fact that I was the handywoman for my apartment building?"

I open my mouth to argue that it's different because Anna's work is now relevant to the kingdom, but she barrels on before I can get a word out.

"Hell no! I would've sent him packing if he acted that way, but he didn't. He applauded what I had achieved because he loved and respected me. If you actually love and respect Ruby, you've got a long way to go to prove it. I'm sure you made her feel like used gum on the bottom of your shoe. Less than."

Bile rises in my throat as Ruby's words come back to me. *You're not better than me just because you do charitable work. Every contribution can be meaningful if it comes from the heart.* Her work means a lot to her, which is all that matters. I ranked her worth below mine when it's not. She's everything to me, above me in the ways that count—open, warm, and loving. And I was wretched to her.

Anna pats my arm. "I can see you're getting it now. Make sure you really grovel." She returns to her seat.

By the time the hired limo pulls up to Ruby's parents' modest one-story peach stucco home in a suburban development, I'm so nervous I can barely think straight. I can't screw this up.

Anna hollers at me on my way out of the car, "Grovel like you mean it!"

I lift a hand in acknowledgment and walk up the front sidewalk. Princes don't grovel. It's not in my DNA. But I will right the wrong, correct course, and say what I should've said the first time around. I love her and that is what will make everything work out. It has to. Of course, it's not at all a sure thing. I didn't call ahead for fear she wouldn't see me.

I'm dressed casually in an aquamarine button-down shirt that matches my eyes (Ruby often complimented my eye color, marveling at it), black trousers, and black leather shoes. I'm carrying a bouquet of roses, which Anna said is a necessary item for the classic grovel. It's my only concession to groveling.

Rafe and Henry stand behind me on the concrete porch, waiting for me to get up the nerve to ring the bell. There's a screen door and a white front door. I debate knocking on one or the other instead of ringing the bell. Damn nerves. I press the bell.

The door opens a few moments later to a petite woman with a short cap of dirty blond hair. This must be Ruby's mother. She leaves the screen door shut and peers through it at me. "Yes?"

I force a smile. "Hello, I'm Phillip Rourke. These are my guards. I'm here to see Ruby."

Her eyes widen. "You're the royal hottie!" She yanks open the screen door, her pregnant stomach large and round under a yellow T-shirt. "Come in before the neighbors get wind of you! Edward, the prince is here! Ruby!"

"Thank you, ma'am." I step into a living room tastefully decorated with a white sofa and matching armchairs, a honey-colored wood coffee table and end tables. I suspect Ruby had something to do with the way the room was pulled together. It looks like something out of a magazine. Elegant in its simplicity.

"Please have a seat," she says, gesturing for us to take the sofa. "I'm Eileen. Eeep! This is so exciting! Your Highness, the royal hottie, right here in my living room!"

I take a seat. "Just Phillip will suffice."

She looks at the guards still standing by the front door and turns back to me. "Can I get you anything?"

"Just Ruby, please."

"I'll be right back!"

The house isn't soundproof in the least, and I can clearly hear her as she rushes down the hallway and hollers, "Edward, hurry up in the bathroom! There's a prince in the living room. Yes! The one Ruby's been bitching about!"

I shift in my seat. Her mother has been very cordial considering her daughter's been bitching about me. I catch Rafe's eye. He and Henry look amused. Nothing like witnesses to your grovel.

A moment later, we hear someone pounding on a door and rattling the knob. Then Eileen hollers, "Unlock the door this minute! Phillip is here to see you!"

I can't hear Ruby's response muffled by the door.

"Ruby Evans, I will unscrew these hinges and pull you out by the hair if you don't get your butt out here!"

Her father chimes in. "That will take too long. I'll go to the window and pull her out that way."

Perhaps her parents are eager to get rid of her. Ruby did say they needed her room for the baby. *That will only help my cause.*

"You're supposed to be on my side!" Ruby hollers.

"We're on your side, sweetheart," her mother says. "But we know how you feel about him. Don't let pride keep you from the man you love."

I leap to my feet. *She loves me!* That's all I need to know. I follow the sounds down the short hallway to Ruby's bedroom.

"Hello, I'm Ruby's father, Edward." Her father, a tall thin man with a receding blond hairline, offers his hand.

I give him a firm handshake. "Nice to meet you, Edward. If you could just give us a few moments of privacy, I'd really like to talk to Ruby."

"Of course!" her mother exclaims, grabbing her husband by the arm and pulling him with her. "We'll be in the kitchen."

Ruby's door opens a moment later. Her hair is up in a messy ponytail, her eyes bleary, her lips drawn into a flat line. She's dressed more casually than I've seen her before in a pink T-shirt with denim shorts, barefoot. She's beautiful, sexy, and seriously pissed off.

I hand her the roses. "I'm sorry."

She takes them and steps back, letting me into her room and shutting the door behind me. The room is vintage teen Ruby and extremely girly—white frilly canopy bed, white dresser and nightstand with flower decals, pink walls, pink carpet. There's a few posters of shirtless rock stars from a decade or so ago arranged on a diagonal on one wall. Even her lusty crushes are arranged in a design. Her parents have left her room here waiting for her if she should need it. I like that she comes from a good family.

She sits on her bed and stares at the roses in her hands.

I remain standing since she hasn't invited me to join her. "Your parents are nice."

She lifts her head. "They're impressed with your royal bloodlines, as is the world. You're a celebrity." She doesn't sound very impressed.

I clear my throat. "I'm sorry for hurting your feelings. I didn't mean to sound so self-righteous. I know your work is important to you, which makes it important to me too. You're great at it."

"But you don't think it's as important as your work."

"It's not a fair comparison. I'm sure once basic needs are met, anyone would appreciate the beauty you bring to the world." My voice catches as the truth of that hits me. "You had it right. Each of us should contribute in the way that's most meaningful to us."

She's quiet, her gaze downcast. I'm losing her, and I can't bear it.

I drop to my knees in front of her, so we're eye to eye, and speak urgently, from the heart. "Ruby, I've had a lot of time to think about it, and I realized I went about this whole thing the wrong way. What I should've said before, what I should've started with is this—I love you." I hold my breath, desperately hoping she'll say it back. If we have love, everything else will work itself out.

She stares at me for a long tense moment.

I still, my heartbeat roaring in my ears, my chest tight.

And then her eyes fill. "Okay," she says quietly.

I can breathe again. She blinks rapidly and tears spill down her cheeks. The sight fills me with hope, my own eyes stinging.

I sit next to her on the bed and wipe her tears with the pad of my thumb. "And I know you love me too."

She laughs a little. "Oh, you do, huh?"

"Your mother was pretty loud when she told you not to let your pride keep you from the man you love. I assumed she meant me, unless you and Rafe…"

She shoves my arm and smiles through her tears. "Stop."

"I've missed you."

She sniffles. "I've missed you too." She meets my eyes. "I do love you."

The tension that's built over the past several days leaves my body in a rush. I pull her into my arms and hug her. "I love hearing you say it."

A moment later, she pulls away. "I was able to secure several clients from Anna's friends when I got back. Actually, three of them are eager for their homes to be done before the New Year and are paying me double to make it happen. I have enough work for six months. I can get my own place with the advance deposits."

"That's great. I'm happy for you. I know that's what you wanted."

She purses her lips. "Only you ruined it. I couldn't enjoy any of it, couldn't even start to apartment shop because I've been miserable without you."

I stroke her hair back from her face. "I've been miserable too."

She exhales sharply. "That doesn't make me feel as good as I thought it would."

"You hoped for my misery?"

"Oh, yeah. I wanted you to be an empty shell of a man cursing the day you lost the best thing to ever happen to you. I hoped you'd become impotent in your grief and never be able to enjoy another woman for the rest of your miserable life."

"Damn, remind me never to get on your bad side again."

She laughs. "I know. I just wanted you to be as miserable as I was. Phillip, you really hurt my feelings. It's like you thought you were so much better than me, that I was being greedy and small-minded while you were taking the higher path. I'd felt so close to you, closer than I've ever felt with anyone, and then it seemed like the gap between us was too great to ever bridge. We do come from different worlds."

"It works for Gabriel and Anna."

"Anna has always longed for a stable foundation and family. Gabriel gave her that. But Phillip, that's not me. I have everything I need right here, except you. I just don't know how we fit."

"I'll move to Tampa." I surprise myself with the impulsive decision, but it's the only way I can think of to keep her happy.

Her jaw drops. "What? You can't move to Tampa. You have to continue your good work. It's important to you and the world."

We stare at each other at an impasse. She wants me to do what I most want to do; she just doesn't want to do that with me. And I don't really belong here. We both know that.

She turns away, and my heart leaps in my throat.

"Ruby."

"Maybe you were right before," she says quietly. "We're on two diverging paths."

"Marry me."

Her head whips toward mine, her green eyes wide.

She looks as surprised as I am, but now that I've said it, I want to. I love her. That's everything. The only thing.

I take both her hands. "I need you in my life, Ruby. Permanently. You are *my* stable foundation, the heart of it, the center of everything I do. I know it's sudden. I don't even have a ring, but there's nothing I want more than you by my side for life."

She looks happy for a moment, but then she frowns. "How does that solve anything?"

"We were asking the wrong question. It's not which job takes precedence. The right question is, how does everything else in our lives fit around us as a couple? We start with love." I give her a quick kiss. "We'll be a unified front, and we'll decide everything together. Where we live, how we live." I frame her beautiful face with my hands. "There's just nothing more important to me than you. None of this means anything without you in my life."

Her brows draw together as her gaze searches mine.

I drop my hands and wait, barely breathing, hoping for the answer I most want to hear.

Her lips purse as she mulls it over. Finally, she says, "I like that a lot. We could set aside blocks of time. Six months here for my career, six months traveling as ambassadors for clean water. You have the pull to get people to work with your schedule, and you could take the occasional trip without me."

I can breathe again, joy spearing through me, making everything feel light and bright. She's on board. "And you'll marry me?"

She smiles cheekily. "When I hear a proposal worthy of Prince Phillip Rourke."

I drop to one knee in front of her and gallantly take her

hand. "Ruby Evans, will you do me the great honor of becoming my wife?"

"Yes!"

She throws herself at me, and I catch her, holding her close for a long moment. She kisses me, and it's the sweetest welcome. Suddenly we're ravenous for each other and tumble to the floor. She's on top of me, and I run my hands all over her petite soft curves.

She lifts her head suddenly. "We should go somewhere more private."

"Yes, and quickly."

She giggles and rushes to the bedroom door, pulling it open. Her parents jump back, looking guilty. "Mom! Dad!"

"Congratulations, sweetheart!" her mother exclaims.

Her father pumps my hand. "Welcome to the family! Do we get to visit the palace?"

14

___

Ruby

Phillip and I are hot for each other, but first things first. We're an engaged couple and my parents are ecstatic. We join them in the kitchen to toast with some chardonnay. Mom, of course, sticks to water.

"Congratulations!" my mother exclaims, clinking glasses with each of us in turn.

"Congratulations," my father says.

Phillip clinks glasses with me last, his eyes never leaving mine as he takes a sip. I do too.

"Well, we should go," I say. "Phillip needs me to drive him back to his hotel, where he can work with his press secretary to get the official royal announcement out."

Phillip sets his glass on the counter, picking up my cue. "Yes, very important that it be done face-to-face, so the news doesn't leak ahead of time."

"Oh, wow!" my mother exclaims. "An official royal announcement! Will you get married here or at the palace?"

"Ruby?" Phillip asks.

I love that he's leaving it up to me, even though I'm sure all royal weddings take place in the chapel at Amalie Palace. That's where Anna and Gabriel got married. My parents recorded it, and we watched it later on TV.

I turn to my parents. "Would it be okay with you if we married at the palace chapel? We'd wait until it was a good time for you to travel with the baby." They still haven't picked a name.

My mom's face lights up with a beaming smile. "We'd love that! Phillip, we saw Anna's wedding on TV. That chapel is so beautiful. Will you have the horse-drawn carriage too?"

Phillip pipes up. "Ruby will have anything she wants."

"He's a keeper," my mom says.

"Yup!" I hug her and then my dad. "I'll call you. We've got so much planning to do."

Phillip shakes both their hands, but my mom insists on hugging him and then kisses his cheek. It didn't take them long to warm to him, considering I called him holier-than-thou, demanding, and arrogant. As a longtime royal hottie follower, my mom always said she thought he must be a sweetheart in real life. She based this solely on his warm smile. Turned out she was right.

We finally make our escape, and I lead him and the guards to the street where my Toyota hatchback has been baking in the Florida sun. I unlock it and fold up the sun visor from the dashboard.

I turn to Rafe and Henry, both over six feet tall, who I know are going to be squished in the backseat. "Sorry. I know it's not the roomy Mercedes you're used to."

"No problem, ma'am," Henry says. Rafe looks grim.

They squish their long muscular frames into the backseat, I hop in the driver's seat, and Phillip slides in the passenger side.

I turn the car on, blast the air conditioner, and turn to Phillip. "Where to?"

"I actually didn't plan that far ahead. I was so focused on fixing things with you that was all I could think about. Anna and Gabriel are staying at the Epicurean Hotel. We could go there."

It's a luxury hotel. This is my life now, tempered with the unusual combination of working in the trenches of the most impoverished communities. A future I never could've imagined for myself, but I know ultimately will be extremely fulfilling. Plus I still have my life back home for half of the year.

"Or wherever you think is good," he adds.

"My, aren't you accommodating now," I tease.

He laughs. "It probably won't last. I'm just so thrilled things went well between us. Better take advantage while you can. I'd pretty much give you anything right now."

There's a loud throat clearing from the backseat.

Phillip turns. "Relationship advice, Rafe?"

"You have a room at the Epicurean, as do we."

"Ah."

Rafe rattles off the address, but I already know it. I grew up here. I drive over to the hotel and hand the keys of my decidedly nonluxury car over to the valet.

Phillip grabs my hand and practically runs to the front desk. Within minutes, we're on our way to the room. His luggage is already there. The guards file into their room next door.

It's a suite, and I barely register the elegant living room before Phillip scoops me up, cradled in his arms, and carries me to the bedroom. Swoon!

"Music," I tell him. "We need some sound so the guards can't hear."

"Oh, Ruby, they don't care. Trust me."

"I care!"

He sets me on my feet by the bed and presses the radio clock on the nightstand. It's top 40 pop and it's loud.

I smile. "Perfect!"

He slides open the nightstand drawer, and a box of condoms is in there. He grunts in approval.

"Eww! We are *not* using leftovers from the last person who stayed here."

He laughs. "These are mine. My valet left them. It's my preferred brand, and see?" He lifts the box to show me a small gold sticker with his initials on the bottom.

My eyes widen. "You have personalized stickers? Like monogrammed condoms?" I laugh.

He grins. "It's his little touch when he leaves me something unanticipated, so I know it's okay. Clearly, he was hoping for our reconciliation."

I stare at him, speechless. Having a public life is going to take some getting used to.

"Would you rather I didn't have them, and then I had to request condoms from the concierge?"

I wrap my arms around his middle. "So you really didn't expect this?"

He wraps his arms around me and gazes down at me. "I wasn't sure if you'd even see me."

"Didn't you know I love you?"

"No. I hoped, but I didn't know. I thought I ruined it."

"Well, I do."

He cradles my face with his hands. "I never thought I'd love again, and then you gallivanted into my life and turned me inside out. I've been walking around with my heart outside my chest, in your hands, since the very first time you were in my arms."

I smile at the memory of our time in the yacht's cabin, my heart filled to bursting. "I am quite the gallivanter."

He speaks against my lips. "Thankfully." And then we're kissing, and there's no more talk. He rips my shirt off, unhooks the bra, and tosses it, openly admiring my breasts as he works the button on my shorts.

A small niggling worry makes me ask, "You don't think I'm too small?" He made a comment about my size during our fight, and I'm a little sensitive about that. "Small body, small-minded."

He closes his eyes for a moment and pulls me tight against him. "You are petite, but I shouldn't have commented on your size. And you're not small-minded either. I so regret saying those things." He pulls back and runs his hands down my sides. "I love your petite curves. You're so beautiful, so sexy, and you fit so perfectly with me."

I lift my chin, still a little miffed. "Maybe the problem is you. Maybe you're too big."

He smirks but says nothing. Instead he undoes my denim shorts and pulls them down along with my panties. Then he pulls back the covers, lifts me by the waist, and tosses me on the bed.

"Ah! Phillip! You can't just toss me around like a doll."

"I like how easy it is to lift you." He grins. "I'll try to restrain myself. Or you could do the same to me." He starts unbuttoning his shirt, looking smug. He knows I could barely move him. He's bigger with at least fifty pounds of muscle on me. There are other ways…

I sit up and undo his pants, quickly freeing him. Then I

take his thick erection in hand. "I can bring you to your knees with one suck."

He grips my hair in one hand, tilting my face up to his. "You could bring me to my knees with one word. I love you so damn much, Ruby. There's nothing I wouldn't do for you."

My jaw drops at the words uttered so sincerely I can't help but believe him. No man has ever felt so strongly about me that they'd do absolutely anything. Most guys did the bare minimum.

He smiles as he pushes me onto my back. "So you see, the power dynamic here is decidedly in your favor." He rolls a condom on and rises over me, nudging my legs apart, fitting himself between them.

"Phillip."

He entwines his fingers with mine and raises my hands above my head, pinning them to the mattress. "Yes, love?"

"No one has ever said anything like that to me in my life."

"Glad to be the first." He slides smoothly inside me, bringing a delicious ache. "Wrap your ankles high on my waist."

The moment I do, he pumps into me, deep and hard and fast. It's exactly what I need. His gaze is locked on mine, the intensity building with every stroke. He slips a hand under me, angling my hips up, taking me deeper. My breath is ragged as I draw closer and closer to the edge. His mouth closes over mine, his body shifting inside me, triggering an intense pleasure. Everything in me coils tight. My head arches back as I break in a rush of pleasure. He keeps pumping, bringing more pleasure. My soft moans turn to a harsh cry as I go over again, and then he lets go, pumping deep, and then finally stilling.

I beam, euphoric, as he gives me his weight. I wrap my arms around him and hug him tight. "I love you, I love you, I love you."

He lifts his head and smiles, kissing me tenderly. "I love you too. Hmm…three I love yous for two orgasms. I think I owe you another orgasm soon." He rolls to his back on the mattress next to me.

I roll to my side, facing him, and prop up on my elbow. "I like the way you think." I run my hand over his heated chest. "And I'm always game for more."

He turns his face toward me and smiles. "Just give me a moment."

I straddle him, reach for the radio and turn it down. He sits up with me in his arms, grabs the covers, and pulls them over both of us as he lies back down. His warm hand strokes down my back, and I rest my hands on his chest and look up at him. His eyes are closed, his expression relaxed. He's got scruff like he forgot to shave, and I love that he was so focused on getting back to me, fixing things between us, that he forgot the basics.

I kiss his chest. "Did you repack your suitcase, or is that suitcase from your last trip?"

"It's from India. I wanted to go straight to you, but I had to stop at home for Anna and Gabriel."

"She told me about Mike. We should go over later."

"Yes. How do you feel about food?"

"I like food."

"Excellent."

An hour later, we're sitting in plush white robes in the small dining area of the suite, enjoying a delicious lunch. And then we make plans—big plans—working out the logistics of our lives as true equals and partners. Everything goes through the filter of *does this allow us to be our best selves together?* Then it's a yes, otherwise no. He's at the center of my life, and I'm at the center of his. Our next stop is back to Villroy for his sister Emma's wedding; then it's off to New York City for a meeting at the UN before heading back to Tampa.

My life will soon be three different roles—the wife of a prince, an interior designer and big sister in Florida, and an ambassador for clean water. I'm not officially an ambassador, but, at my request, Phillip will be putting me in charge of spearheading efforts for girls and education. That's my special project, and I love it.

"What about kids?" he asks. "I'd definitely like kids."

I sit up straight, joy spreading through me. "Yes to kids, after we're done travelling. Maybe when I'm thirty. Is that okay?" I know he's twenty-nine. I'm asking him to wait five years.

"Absolutely. How many?"

"My mom had a lot of miscarriages. I'm not sure how it will go for me."

He takes my hand across the table. "If there's any difficulty, we could always adopt. We've seen all the orphans left behind in devastated areas."

My throat chokes. He's such a good man, and he's right. "I love that idea. Yes. In that case, four kids."

He grins. "I grew up with six brothers and sisters. Big families are fun. We'll have help too. Maybe my old nanny will be willing to join our family."

"If she's not busy with Anna and Gabriel's baby."

"She's pregnant?"

"Not that I heard, but she told me they're working on it."

He snorts. "Working on it. Like fucking could ever be work." He stands. "C'mere, I need you for very fun purposes. Notice how I didn't just pick you up like a doll?"

"Good thing! I just ate. Never toss around a fiancée with a full stomach."

He holds out his hand to me. "Ruby."

I stand and take his hand. He gives me a tug, pulling me into his arms and kissing me. Then he dips his head, his voice a rumble in my ear, "We're going to play a game. It's called screaming orgasm."

I smile up at him. "I like this game."

He cups my cheek. "I know you do. I invented it in your honor."

"You can carry me to the bedroom."

He scoops me up, cradled in his arms. "So you like that, do you?"

I nod. "It's romantic."

He sets me down inside the bedroom, shuts the door, and lifts me so we're eye to eye, pinning me against the door. I wrap my arms and legs around him. "You and me, Ruby, from here on out. Forever."

"Yes," I manage over the lump in my throat. I've never known a man who expressed himself so warmly, so lovingly before. He's got a big heart.

His lips meet mine, and my mind shuts down, lost in sensation. Long moments later, he sets me back on my feet and rips my robe off. I rip his off too. He snags a condom from the robe pocket.

"So prepared!" I exclaim.

"I have to be when I'm around you." He finishes rolling it on, grabs me by the waist, lifts me, and impales me onto him. My breath shudders out, and I wrap my legs around his waist, the wall at my back. He uses his grip on my hips, lifting me as he pounds into me. "The advantage of your size," he rasps. "I can lift you like this."

"Don't stop."

And then I go over, my body shuddering around him. He's got me tight, thrusting over and over. Soft cries escape as the pleasure builds again. He angles me back, his hand sliding between us, stroking me. White-hot sensations rip through me. I dig my fingernails into his shoulders, the intensity nearly unbearable. And then I explode, the scream ripped from my throat. I'm wrecked, collapsed against him, as he thrusts for his own release and slams deep into me one last time, moaning into the side of my neck.

He lifts his head and kisses me tenderly. Then he turns, still holding me, and walks us to the bed, setting me gently down on the mattress before joining me. He rolls me to my side away from him and then spoons his big warm body behind me. I let out a sigh of pure contentment. I don't mind him maneuvering my body when he does it for these sexy and loving positions.

He brushes my hair back from my face and whispers in my ear, "The guards know what you sound like now when you let go, so you can feel free to let go without worrying about them storming the room."

I freeze. *WHAT?* "Phillip?"

"Mmm-hmm." His arm bands around my waist, pinning me tight against him like I might leap out of bed and ream him. I'm too spent for that.

I keep my voice level. "Did we play the screaming orgasm game for the guards' benefit?"

"No, darling, that was for you."

I relax a little.

"That was just a convenient side benefit."

"Phillip!" I glare at him over my shoulder.

He kisses me. "Now thank me for your screaming orgasm."

I huff and lie back on my side.

His fingers slide between my legs, and I moan. "Was that a thank-you I heard?" he teases.

"You will pay," I growl, and then I gasp. He owns my body, and I love it.

A long while later, I melt into the mattress, spent. He's dedicated himself quite thoroughly solely to my pleasure. "Thank you."

"There it is!" he crows, lifting his head from between my legs. He shifts to sit next to me on the mattress. "I knew I could get it out of you if I just put my mind to it. And my lips and tongue—"

I prop up on my elbows and glare at him. "Shhh!"

"You still haven't learned your lesson? No inhibitions because of the guards." He sighs. "We'll have to start again."

I sit up and tackle him. He lets me, falling to his back. Then I kiss him all over his scruffy face.

His cheeks curve against my lips. "That's more like it." And then he just holds me, his arms wrapped tight around me.

I rest my head on his chest, listening to the steady thump of his heart. I'm exactly where I want to be, where I was meant to be, surrounded by love.

EPILOGUE

The following week in the royal dining room...

Phillip

I'm bursting to tell my family the big news of our engagement, but I have to wait. We're gathered at my sister Emma's rehearsal dinner with her fiancé, Abdul, who is from a small kingdom in Southeast Asia. Their wedding is tomorrow at the chapel here, and Emma will go to live with him after their marriage. He's rather bland, very proper like our Emma, and seems nice enough. His dark brown hair is neatly parted to the side, and he's wearing a navy blue suit with a rose-colored tie and pocket square. Emma matches him, wearing a modest long-sleeved rose dress with a string of pearls. Her long dark brown hair is neatly parted down the middle, her big hazel eyes downcast, her demeanor subdued and rather stiff, her full pink lips pressed into a tight line. I really thought she'd look happier on the occasion she's waited so many years for. Maybe she's nervous. She and Abdul were an arranged marriage set up by our mutual king-doms. She accepted him as her future husband when she was sixteen and had to wait until she turned twenty-five to wed, according to my parents' wishes. She turned twenty-five last week. The fact that she rarely indulges in alcohol and has definitely had some champagne should've relaxed her.

Maybe it's because our mother isn't here. She's become a recluse, taking her meals in her room. She says she'll be at the wedding tomorrow, which will be her first public appearance since my father died. Ruby and I visited her in her suite and told her our big news earlier. She gave us her blessing, though she didn't seem excited. Not much can penetrate the thick cloud of grief that surrounds her. I understand. She's lost the love of her life.

As soon as the meal is finished, I stand and walk around to where Emma is seated next to her fiancé. Abdul's parents and his two sisters are here, as well as all of my siblings. "Congratulations to you both."

"Thank you, Phillip," Emma says in a near monotone.

I check her eyes. She's not drunk. I've never seen her drunk, but her behavior is so at odds with the happy occasion I wondered if alcohol has a subduing effect on her. Actually, she looks like she checked out. Her eyes are blank.

"Thank you," Abdul says in perfect English. "I'm pleased we can finally move forward now that Emma has reached the proper age."

"Yes, happy birthday, little sister." I was away at the time.

She barely inclines her head.

I give her shoulder a squeeze. "Would it be okay if I shared some good news with our family, or should I wait for a different occasion? I don't want to take away from your celebration."

"Oh, no, please go ahead," Emma says.

I turn to Abdul, who gestures for me to go ahead.

I head over to Ruby, lean down, and whisper, "I'm going to tell them our news."

She smiles and nods.

I clink a spoon against a glass and the room quiets, my brothers and sisters all turning their attention to me. Gabriel and Anna are here too. She's not quite herself after losing Mike last week. He died within an hour of her arrival. It seems he'd been hanging on just to say goodbye. She arranged for a quiet funeral, as he'd wanted, and returned home.

I take everyone in. "On this most happy occasion, I want to extend a warm congratulations to Emma and Abdul."

Everyone applauds and murmurs their congratulations. My siblings are less than enthusiastic. They think Emma took the proper princess thing too far, agreeing to an arranged marriage. It was an option my parents broached for all of us. Only Gabriel and Emma would even consider it. They're two peas in a proper royal pod. I could see it with Gabriel, the heir, but Emma is fifth in line for the throne. She just believed it important to carry on tradition, probably because my proper mother emphasized the point. Those two were always very close. Emma was the daughter my mother hoped for after having four sons.

I go on. "And I have some more happy news I'd like to share." I smile down at my beloved. Her cheeks flush pink. I turn back to the group. "Ruby and I are engaged."

Everyone cheers, my brothers whistling and hooting. I lean down and kiss Ruby's smiling, blushing cheek.

Once the noise dies down, she lifts a hand. "Thank you, everyone. We're very happy."

Anna comes around to hug us both. "Congratulations! Ruby, I'm so, so glad everything worked out. I hope this means you'll live here on Villroy."

"Actually," Ruby says, "we're going to be travelling for my work and his, shifting around for a while. Probably until we're ready to settle down to raise a family."

"I wish you so much happiness," Anna says, her voice more subdued. She gives us a watery smile.

Gabriel pops out of his seat, comes over to congratulate us, and then guides Anna back to her chair.

I catch Emma's eye. "Congratulations," she says tightly.

"Thank you, and congratulations to you too. You must be so excited the big day is tomorrow."

Abdul listens intently to her answer.

She smiles, but it doesn't reach her eyes. "Of course. It's taken quite a lot of planning, and now it's finally here."

"Nine years," Abdul says. "That's a long time to wait."

"Right," I say. "Well, we're all looking forward to it."

Gabriel and Anna take their leave soon after while the rest of us go to the parlor to continue the party. It's the second week of November and too cool to go up to the rooftop garden. Emma excuses herself promptly at nine, as is her custom, sticking to her usual bedtime. She has a strict schedule for everything, a strict routine of her own devising. I hope marriage loosens her up, though from the look of Abdul, also neat and proper, maybe it'll just be more of the same. Hell, what do I know? Maybe that's what she needs.

The next day, I walk with Ruby toward the palace chapel, where Emma will soon be married. Ruby wanted to take a peek before the ceremony and look around. Probably wants to take pictures too. She does love historic architecture and design. And I love her more than I ever thought possible. Last night we all stayed up late in the parlor, drinking and chatting, so my siblings had a chance to get to know Ruby. Each of them, in turn, let me know they thought Ruby was perfect for me. I couldn't agree more.

I take Ruby's hand, entwining our fingers together. She turns to me and smiles, her green eyes bright. I smile back, an ebullient joy filling me as I think of our shared future. I wonder where we'll ultimately land for a permanent home. At the palace? A separate home on Villroy? Maybe in nearby France? Or in the US? I consider different locations and ways this could work, especially with children. Wherever it is, our home will be filled with love.

I spot Gabriel and Anna in the hallway dressed in their formal wear of a black tux and peach gown respectively, appearing quite the elegant duo. "Hello," I call cheerfully. "Beautiful day for a wedding."

Gabriel stalks toward me, his expression grim. Anna hurries to catch up with him. I'm instantly on alert. Maybe something's wrong with Mother. Maybe she's too upset to come out of her rooms for the wedding after all. This will devastate Emma. They've always been close.

"What is it?" I ask.

"Emma's gone missing," Gabriel whispers urgently. "Have you seen her?"

"No. Did you check with Silvia?" Our sister planned to help Emma get ready.

"Of course I checked with Silvia," he snaps. "She said Emma was in her gown and asked for a moment to herself. When Silvia went back to the room, she was gone."

"It's a big palace," Ruby says. "She must be around here somewhere. Maybe she's visiting with your mother."

"Yes, that," I say, turning to Ruby with a smile. "You're brilliant."

"She's not with Mother," Gabriel says through his teeth. "We checked. We need to spread out and scour the palace without raising any alarms."

I nod. "Ruby and I will take the east wing. You and Anna take the west wing."

"Do you think she bailed on her wedding?" Ruby whispers.

Gabriel lifts his chin and says in a haughty voice, "Of course not. She's likely lost track of time due to pre-wedding nerves. Nothing serious. We'll reassure her and all will be well."

"Actually," Anna says slowly.

We all turn to her.

A muscle ticks in Gabriel's jaw as he waits for his wife to finish her sentence.

Anna grimaces. "She *might* have taken me up on my suggestion to get away and think."

Gabriel shakes his head, frowning.

"Oh, so she's taking a walk," I say. "That's a relief."

"It's worse than that," Gabriel says in a low voice. "Isn't it, Anna?"

Anna instantly flushes guiltily. He knows her so well. "Don't worry. She's safe."

"You couldn't have done something before her wedding day?" Gabriel asks tightly.

Anna gestures wildly. "I tried, but your sister is as stubborn as you and set in her ways. I merely gave her an option, which I did yesterday. She's the one who chose now to take it."

Gabriel looks alarmed and immediately rushes toward the side door that leads outside, probably to track down Emma.

"Gabriel!" Anna calls, rushing over to him.

He stops, and they have a heated conversation that I can't make out from here, and then Gabriel strides outside, Anna hot on his heels.

Who would've thought my proper sister would be a runaway bride?

"Never a dull moment around here," Ruby quips.

I slide an arm around her shoulders and hold her close. "Welcome to my world."

She smiles up at me. "I love it, and I love you."

I kiss her. "I love you too."

She rubs my chest. "And here I thought royal life was so staid and proper."

"It is, and it isn't."

"Are you worried about her?"

"It's an island. How far could she get?"

Don't miss the next book in the series *Royal Darling*, where Emma and a British bad boy rock star collide!

Jackson

Being a rock god isn't all it's cracked up to be. It's become a soulless grind. Which is why I'm now on my mate's houseboat, far away from the spotlight, hoping to find my way back to the music. Yeah. Not gonna happen.

I've just discovered a stowaway on board, and I can't believe who she is. A bloody princess? And the prim little woman won't leave the boat, so I make an offer to scare her off—a no-strings fling.

Only she says yes.

I say no, and she promptly locks herself in my bedroom.

I swear I'm dropping her off at the next port.

She's trouble wrapped in a pretty virginal package, and I know I shouldn't touch.

Emma

I'm a runaway bride trying to make a clean escape. But when Jackson Walker discovers me hiding on his boat—after I get over the shock of stumbling upon a rock star's hideaway—I immediately know he's exactly what I need. He's wild, rough around the edges, *perfect*.

My family would never approve. The press would skewer us. I still want him.

He's the antidote to my tightly prescribed life.

But can he ever see past my title to the woman I long to be?

Sign up for my newsletter to be emailed when *Royal Darling* releases at kyliegilmore.com/newsletter

ALSO BY KYLIE GILMORE

Happy Endings Book Club Series

Hidden Hollywood (Book 1)

Inviting Trouble (Book 2)

So Revealing (Book 3)

Formal Arrangement (Book 4)

Bad Boy Done Wrong (Book 5)

Mess With Me (Book 6)

Resisting Fate (Book 7)

Chance of Romance (Book 8)

Wicked Flirt (Book 9)

An Inconvenient Plan (Book 10)

A Happy Endings Wedding (Book 11)

The Clover Park Series

The Opposite of Wild (Book 1)

Daisy Does It All (Book 2)

Bad Taste in Men (Book 3)

Kissing Santa (Book 4)

Restless Harmony (Book 5)

Not My Romeo (Book 6)

Rev Me Up (Book 7)

An Ambitious Engagement (Book 8)

Clutch Player (Book 9)

A Tempting Friendship (Book 10)

Clover Park Bride: A Clover Park Short

A Valentine's Day Gift (Book 11)

Maggie Meets Her Match (Book 12)

The Clover Park STUDS Series

Almost Over It (Book 1)

Almost Married (Book 2)

Almost Fate (Book 3)

Almost in Love (Book 4)

Almost Romance (Book 5)

Almost Hitched (Book 6)

The Rourkes Series

Royal Catch (Book 1)

Royal Hottie (Book 2)

Royal Darling (Book 3)

Royal Charmer (Book 4)

Royal Player (Book 5)

Royal Shark (Book 6)

ABOUT THE AUTHOR

Kylie Gilmore is the *USA Today* bestselling author of the Rourkes series, the Happy Endings Book Club series, the Clover Park series, and the Clover Park STUDS series. She writes humorous romance that makes you laugh, cry, and reach for a cold glass of water.

Kylie lives in New York with her family, two cats, and a nutso dog. When she's not writing, wrangling kids, or dutifully taking notes at writing conferences, you can find her flexing her muscles all the way to the high cabinet for her secret chocolate stash.

Thanks for reading *Royal Hottie*. I hope you enjoyed it. Would you like to know about new releases? You can sign up for my new release email list at kyliegilmore.com/newsletter. I promise not to clog your inbox! Only new release info, sales, and some fun giveaways.

I love to hear from readers! You can find me at:
  kyliegilmore.com
  Instagram.com/kyliegilmore
  Facebook.com/KylieGilmoreToo
  Twitter @KylieGilmoreToo

If you liked Phillip and Ruby's story, please leave a review on your favorite retailer's website or Goodreads. Thank you.

www.ingramcontent.com/pod-product-compliance
Lightning Source LLC
Chambersburg PA
CBHW070947180726
48291CB00004B/1178